THE NEW YORKERS

BY JAYNE LOUISE CRAMFORDE AND RICHARD BONTE

JAYNE LOUISE CRAMFORDE AND RICHARD BONTE

The year is 1917, the end of the Gilded Era in New York, the drums of war sounding in Europe. A beautiful young socialite with a perfect life—whose only problem is which successful tycoon to marry—seduces a man who may destroy her future.

PROLOGUE

1925

Celia Casterson was seated outside on the deck of the *SS Normandie*, the most French of all French steamships, a floating Château de Versailles. At sixty thousand tons and one thousand feet in length, this magnificent ship sped along at twenty-five knots, cutting through the dark blue of the Atlantic, one thousand miles from its destination of Liverpool. A few days before, Mrs. Casterson had embarked in New York where she had attended several different gala events. Now, Celia was on her way to meet her husband, Don Casterson, who was on business in Liverpool. Celia didn't like to say it, but she welcomed this time away from Don—*I adore Don, I really do,* she always told herself—so she could immerse herself in the "Frenchiness" of the *SS*

Normandie. She had dined in the ship's "Hall of Mirrors," which was an exact copy of the original hall in the Château de Versailles. Celia was one of the ship's 848 first-class passengers, and she shared a three-apartment deluxe suite adjoining the eighty-foot indoor pool with her nanny, and daughter, Sammy. The two of them were now taking a nap after a particularly epicurean lunch. But not Celia. Celia found herself alone, alone with her past and thoughts.

Celia was in love with everything French, from French gastronomy to French culture and language. Everything French for Celia was the most important thing in the world. She took classes in French, studied its gastronomy and viniculture, and bought up the latest in French fashion. In a way, Celia the Francophile was being practical because one could never predict the future. If it didn't work out with Don, she told herself, she might even marry a Frenchman. She was still very young.

She looked up at the swirl of steam above the three funnels of the *SS Normandie* and suddenly noticed that an errant cloud had formed the letter "M" in the sky. She sat up suddenly and stared at the precise formation of this "M" cloud and wondered what it was telling her. What did the "M" stand for? "Magnificent? *Magnifique?* Messiah?" Or was it a sign from "Masters," Jimmy Masters? She had been thinking of him a lot these past few days. Even the different Frenchmen she had dined with couldn't match Masters' manner, his looks, his unforgettable style. *Oh*, she sighed, *I feel so sad thinking about you, Jimmy.*

The wind had picked up and distorted the "M" cloud somewhat. Celia saw this as a sign for her to move inside and compose a letter to her cousin Richard. She sat down at her dresser and began to write. Her fountain pen moved smoothly over the *SS Normandie* thick bond paper.

"My Dearest Richard" she began, "I am writing to you from the wonderful steamship *Normandie.* The captain tells us we are currently one thousand miles away from Liverpool, but the ship is sailing so fast, we could be there any day now. 'We,' as in Nanny, Sammy, and myself, I mean. Personally, I love being all alone in the middle of nowhere in the Atlantic, without a care in the world and looking up at the vast expanse of blue nothingness. Did you know I just saw the letter "M" formed by a cloud in the sky, which made me think of our dear James?"

Celia moistened her lower lip with her tongue as she wrote this, sighed, dipped her gold nib in the jet-black ink, and continued,

"I am so profoundly sorry we were unable to stay for the funeral, but as you know, Don's business affairs demanded his full attention in England. We're going to meet him now actually. And I don't need to remind you that I am determined to make our marriage a great success, as was the case for my parents." Celia twitched as her fountain pen trembled with what it was about to write,

"How can I say this? That story Geri Southern related to you about my knowing Masters in Wichita back in 1917 was untrue. The lieutenant from Camp Chandler whom she thought was Masters was someone else I had been seeing. It was not that Geri had lied. She was simply mistaken. And then there was the account of that summer you told me about, that James told you, yes, that story was merely a figment of his imagination. You remember how his recollections were liable to change depending on his mood? And do you recall I spent the spring of 1917 with my uncle in New York? Dear Richard, you may start hearing some awful stories about me when I was younger, but I implore you to give me the benefit of the doubt.
Your loving cousin, Celia"

Celia did not know whether to end her letter — 'benefit of the doubt'—with a question mark or an exclamation mark, so she ended it with a period. She carefully folded the letter, slipped it inside an envelope, and sealed it with some sealing wax and her signet ring. She looked up from the felt writing area on her Louis XV desk and contemplated her reflection in the antique mirror. It was as if her limpid blue eyes were looking through a box of old letters. Celia searched for something she already knew about but didn't want to uncover. It was a secret from not so long ago. Did it have anything to do with the "M" cloud she had just seen in the sky?

Celia stared at herself in the mirror and began to recall those far-off days. Had they been real or were they just a bad dream?

JAYNE LOUISE CRAMFORDE AND RICHARD BONTE

CHAPTER ONE – JAMES METZ

New York, Upper East Side, Spring 1917

A block from his important job interview, the young man extinguished his cigarette with the toe of his hobnailed boots, adjusted his flat cap, straightened his suspenders, and popped a mint. He would grind and swallow this mint by the time he rang the doorbell of the swanky Fifth Avenue mansion on Manhattan's Upper East Side.

He rang the bell but felt very self-conscious as an old woman appeared on the porch and stared at his second-hand clothes and coarse hands. Then, she nodded roughly at him, and he followed her into a chilly back office where an old man was seated behind an immense ornate desk. The man used his chin to point to an area ten feet away from him where the young man was to stand.

The young man found himself sweating along his hairline. The perspiration ran down his forehead and stung his eyes as he stood there for the longest time. His armpits and the back of his neck were sticky, too.

"It's not hot outside," blurted the old man.

"I'm sorry?" replied the candidate.

"You're sweating, but it's not hot outside. It's cold. It's even cold in here. Are you alright?"

"Fine, sir," said the young man, suddenly twisting his neck and trying to adjust his loose-fitting collar.

The old man stared at the young man for quite some time. Then he said, "Where were you born?"

"Minnesota, sir."

"It's cold up there. Do you sweat like this up there, too?"

"No, sir."

"And your father? What does he do?"

"He's a farmer, sir."

"A farmer! That's a worthy profession. And why don't you remain on his farm?"

"I wanted to better myself, sir."

"That's admirable of you, but aren't you letting your father down in doing so?"

What's wrong with my body? The young man's clean clothes were now soaking wet, and he was starting to feel faint. He was about to topple over when there was a knock at the door.

"Who is it?"

A young woman with deep blue eyes and flaxen hair entered and stared at him. Transfixed, he gazed rudely back. Then, she looked at the old man.

"Yes, my dear?"

"Oh Uncle, I'm so sorry to interrupt but Auntie Betty wanted to know if you would be joining us?"

She again glanced at the young man and blushed a deep red. She turned to her uncle and nodded back at the visitor and said, "Um, is he joining us for afternoon tea, too?"

"No, Celia. Please ask the cook to send my tea here. And please close the door as you leave."

"Yes, of course, Uncle."

The old man glanced at a list of questions on his desk. He had forgotten his unanswered query and went on to the next item on his agenda,

"Now, where was I? Ah yes, this name 'Metz' that you go by? Where does it originate? Germany?"

"I don't know, sir."

"Don't know! How can you not know where your forebears come from? Are you possibly hiding something?"

Metz began to sweat again as he tried to conjure up an appropriate response. It was 1917 and Germany was not popular with the public. It had been blamed for starting the ongoing European war three years earlier. With no regard for the consequences of his answer, Metz decided on honesty,

"Umm, err, yes sir. I believe they were immigrants from Germany." Metz now assumed that he had lost this job, so he was surprised at the old man's answer.

"They are a good solid nation, Metz, not like those awful French. We should be supporting the Germans. What is your first name, Metz?"

"Jimmy, sir. Uhh, I mean James, uh, sir."

The old man smirked slightly, and James sighed with relief. He was elated to still be in the game. There was another knock on the door. "Come in," the old man barked.

James Metz had expected to see the old woman who had first greeted him, or maybe this certain 'Auntie Betty,' but instead it was the old man's blue-eyed niece with natural blond, flaxen hair. She glanced at Metz again as she placed the silver tray filled with tea, watercress sandwiches, and chocolate cake on her uncle's desk. Then, she poured the old man tea and added a little milk to it.

"Thank you, Celia."

Celia smiled at her uncle and glanced furtively back at Metz. Then, she walked slowly to the door and looked back at Metz again. Metz was puzzled. *What is going on? Is she smiling at me? Not a smile from the niece of one of the wealthiest men in New York? No, I must be mistaken. She's probably laughing at me.*

Metz suddenly remembered that he had skipped breakfast as he watched the old man sip his tea and bite into a sandwich.

"Now, where was I? Oh yes, you are German and so, I assume, Lutheran, and hopefully not Catholic. Metz, Metz, Metz," the old man repeated to himself softly. "Oh, my God, you're not a Jew, are you?"

"No, sir, I don't know what we were. There was only one church in the nearest town, and that's where we went on Sunday."

"I see. Well, I assume you will be attending church here in New York. Where is it that you're living?"

"Hester Street, sir."

"That's an immigrant area. Is it Italian, Irish, or Jewish?"

There was another knock on the door.

"Now what!" the old man shouted.

Metz' heart leapt. He was hoping to see the niece—*Celia, was it?* — but it was yet another woman who remained at the open door and said, "We're going for a walk in the park."

"Of course, my dear," said the old man. "Have a good walk. I'm so sorry I shouted at you."

The woman smiled and nodded at the two men and closed the door. The interruption had caused the old man to swivel around, and it was only then that Metz noticed his inquisitor was seated in a wheelchair. He

13

turned back to level Metz with a long stare. A twenty-second stare.

"You have been recommended due to your mechanical knowledge and ability to drive an automobile. I have your address. You will be informed of my decision in due course. Good day, Metz. I assume you can find your own way out."

CHAPTER TWO – THE YALIE

Central Park, New York City

They came upon a narrow inlet of water north of the Ramble, in Central Park. It was mid-spring, and the trees were covered in green. Celia and her aunt sat down heavily on a park bench located near a small bridge over the water.

"Just needed to catch my breath a bit," said Betty. "Not getting any younger, you know."

"Oh, come on, Auntie, look at that beautiful mallard over there, that drake, standing proudly with his emerald-green head erect above his brown coat and white collar," said Celia. "He doesn't need to sit down. He's all by himself." The aunt and her niece contemplated a sole drake perched on a large rock on the edge of the water.

"I wouldn't count on it." said Betty, "He's probably got a big family nearby and he's standing watch. You know, brown mother duck and her ducklings are probably lurking behind that bridge. Which reminds

15

me, we've really got to do something about planning your future. Your mother and I have discussed this at some length."

"Oh? What do you two have in mind?"

"Well, we're referring, of course, who you're going to marry."

"Oh-h, and who might that be? Is he around here? Is he the handsome friend of that drake?"

"Don't be silly, dear," said Aunt Betty, "Your uncle would like you to be introduced to a Yale man, of course."

"And ... not you?" said Celia. She could sense the reluctance in her aunt's voice.

"Well, it's silly, really. Your uncle is far too restrictive in his thinking. After all, what is wrong with a Harvard man?"

"Nothing, I agree. Isn't that like six of one, half a dozen of the other?"

"Not really," said Aunt Betty. "The Yalie your uncle has in mind is Don Casterson."

Celia smiled. She had seen Don three years earlier when he played football. She had been impressed because he was the quarterback of the Yale team. He was so handsome standing there in his white and blue Yale uniform. A bit like the good-looking drake with his emerald-green head and white collar, still poised on the bank of the pond. But then Don's and the drake's image faded, replaced by that of the handsome young man

standing in her uncle's study earlier. The man Uncle
George had interviewed to be their driver and mechanic.
She shook her head as if to erase all these images and ran
to the drake, who flew away in fright to rejoin his large
family. Aunt Betty had been right. A brown mother duck
suddenly paddled into the picture with five ducklings in
tow.

    "You see?" Betty smiled.

    Celia did see. "I guess you were right, Auntie.
The mother has hatched her eggs. Look at those beautiful
little ducklings. They are so small. And there's no ugly
one out there!"

JAYNE LOUISE CRAMFORDE AND RICHARD BONTE

CHAPTER THREE – THE OFFICER

Bergdorf Goodman Department Store, New York City

Bergdorf Goodman was doing its usual thriving business with people rushing here and there, picking up articles to examine. Celia was shopping with her aunt and had her eye on a soldier who stood out in his officer's uniform. She watched him pick up a pair of brown leather gloves, study them, and put them back down. Her aunt's voice brought her out of her reverie.

"Good morning, Mrs. Green," her aunt said to an attractive lady standing next to the army officer.

"Good morning, Mrs. Davenport," said Mrs. Green to Aunt Betty.

"You know my niece, Celia, don't you?" said Aunt Betty. "She's staying with us for a few months."

"Actually, I don't," said Mrs. Green. "Hello Celia, nice to meet you."

"And it's nice to meet you too, Mrs. Green," said Celia.

"Have you met my son, Michael?" said Mrs. Green.

"Oh, hello. Name's Michael Green," said the army officer. He locked eyes with Celia and said, "How are you liking New York?"

"I love it, but I don't know it very well."

"Well, perhaps I can show you around the city some time?"

"I would love that, Mr. Green," said Celia. "I see you're in the army."

"Not yet, Celia. I'm in officer training at Yale. Ready for when the U.S. enters the war."

"Oh dear, I hope not just yet," said Aunt Betty. "But thank you, Michael, for offering to show Celia around. You're very kind. And please, both of you, call us when you have time."

Betty then looked at her watch and said, "Well, Mrs. Green and Michael, it was wonderful meeting you. We will be off now. Hope you find what you were looking for. See you soon."

"Good-bye, Mrs. Green. Good-bye, Mr. Green," said Celia. And no sooner were the words out of her mouth that Betty whisked her niece away. Celia, however, was like a dog on a leash, looking back at another dog she had happened to cross. Michael, for his part, seemed disappointed.

When they were out of earshot, Celia said, "Why did you take me away so quickly?"

"Never be too eager to stick around," said Auntie Betty. "Always keep them guessing. Part of the mystery of being a beautiful woman. Don't worry. I saw the way he looked at you. He'll be calling you soon."

JAYNE LOUISE CRAMFORDE AND RICHARD BONTE

CHAPTER FOUR – THE NICE JEWISH BOY

Manhattan, Lower East Side

James Metz wiped his brow and left a trace of grease under his hairline. He had been working fixing bicycles for a friend and his hands were filthy. He was happy nevertheless because he had been able to make a dollar that day. He trudged up the steps to the tenement flat on Hester Street where he lived with other lodgers. One of them, Richard "Lefty" Goldstein, flew out the door and almost knocked him over.

"Hey Lefty," said Metz, "where ya goin' like that?"

"What's it to you? I'm late for graveyard duty," said Lefty.

"For Chrissake, can't you work during the day like the rest of us?"

"I'm workin' all the time, Metz, not like some of us." And with that, Lefty took off on the run. Metz just shook his head. Then, he went inside and ran into Mrs. Lubelski, his overweight, middle-aged landlady.

"You see that, Mrs. Lubelski? Lefty's doin' graveyard. He's got two good jobs now. What about me? How am I going to pay my rent? I just got odd jobs."

"Maybe not for long? Look what I've got here. A letter for Jimmy!" The envelope was expensive, and elegant handwriting spelled out, "Mr. James Metz."

"Hold on, Mrs. Lubelski, let me wash my hands before I touch that envelope." He returned minutes later, and Mrs. Lubelski was walking back and forth impatiently.

"Come on, Jimmy, I'm waiting." She handed him a knife to open the letter.

James opened the letter carefully, and Mrs. Lubelski thrust her head over it, obscuring James' view of his own letter. "(Reading) 'I am pleased to inform you...' You got it, Jimmy!" she screamed. "Isn't that the job you wanted in the posh area on Fifth Avenue?"

"Yes, Ma'am."

"Aren't ya happy?"

"Of course, I am, Mrs. Lubelski. Of course. Let's have a drink."

"I've got some gefilte fish, too. Would you like that? Let's have a party."

Moments later, Mrs. Lubelski returned with the gefilte fish and some beer. She spread out the food and drink for James and said, "So, Jimmy, now ya got your job, ya should be looking for a wife, no?"

"A wife?"

"Hannah? Hannah!" Mrs. Kubelski called out in a loud voice to someone in a back bedroom, "Where are you? Come and talk to Jimmy."

A skinny, seventeen-year-old girl with pasty white skin moved toward him reluctantly. Mrs. Lubelski pulled her close and held her, almost like an offering, to James. Metz smiled at the girl and said, "Hello, Hannah, how are you today?"

Hannah ran from the room.

"How do you like that?" said Mrs. Lubelski. I offer her a man, and she runs away like a schlemiel. She's seventeen, not five! Jimmy, tell me, a nice Jewish boy like you should be thinking of his future. A man needs a good Jewish wife. No shiksas please, no goy. Now, you listen to Mrs. Lubelski, sweety."

James looked her straight in the eyes and smiled disarmingly as his mind contemplated the lie that was James Metz. *Well, maybe it's not really a lie.* When James Metz arrived in New York, the only room he could afford was in Mrs. Lubelski's property and when she said, "I hope you're Jewish," James knew what he had to say.

JAYNE LOUISE CRAMFORDE AND RICHARD BONTE

CHAPTER FIVE – THE PLAZA

Union Station, New York City

Don Casterson was 210 pounds and 6'2" of muscle. His face was square and chiseled, and his features were symmetrical. This handsome 'bull of a man' was an ex-Yale quarterback who possessed a pedigree in sports and business. Until now, it had been his destiny to improve his father's business through the countless generations of Castersons in Chicago. But would he stay in Chicago, or could he do better in New York? He decided to find out.

After a long train ride from his hometown, he arrived in New York City. He loved Union Station in south Manhattan featuring statues of former American heroes like George Washington on a horse; Abraham Lincoln; and even the esteemed Marquis de Lafayette, the French general without whom there would have been no United States. He considered the Windy City far inferior to New York from every point of view. Today, he was especially happy to see his parents whom he had not seen for a while. They had also come to New York City to visit. He expected they would be with their old friends, the Davenports, and would bring along their cute little niece Celia. However, he hoped she was no longer the silly little thing he had remembered.

He jumped from the train, as it had now drawn to a crawl, and walked briskly outside. There was a fleet of yellow cabs with their large wheels and distinctive spare tire on the side. He took the first one in the taxi queue.

"The Plaza Hotel," said Don to the driver who only grunted at him in response. Don had the feeling that all his senses were alive when he arrived in New York. As the taxi made its way through Union Station and the streets of Greenwich village, he could still smell the remains of the morning food markets on this cold spring day.

The taxi navigated up lower Fifth Avenue, past 34th Street and its grand department stores. Block by block, Don could see the landscape change, from the garment racks and poor areas of lower Fifth, through Hell's Kitchen, and finally to Central Park South. This was the start of the posh area of the Upper East Side. Don Casterson was all about posh in everything he did. His attitude was formed by his father who used to say, "Go first class, boy, or don't go at all."

The Plaza Hotel on the southeast corner of Central Park finally came into view. The iconic 'P' letters on the heart-shaped crest of the Plaza were bathed in gold. The Plaza had been a notable Manhattan landmark when it was first built in the 1880s, but with the 1907 rebuild—that had taken twenty-seven months and $12.5 M to complete—it was magnificent. Just the view of it made Don happy as he jumped out of the cab and left the driver no tip.

Don had always dreamt about his own grandeur. He thought about how he would become one of the 'big men', people like real estate tycoon, Harry S. Black, or John Gates, who had built the Plaza.

Don handed his bag off to a bellboy. Then, he strutted into the lobby and contemplated an ornate grand staircase, a row of ten elevators, and one of the 1,650 Plaza chandeliers that took his breath away.

Not seeing his parents, he was about to sit down and have a scotch at the bar next to the crowded main lobby. There were dozens of people everywhere. Being taller than most, he was able to look over the crowd and spot people quickly. He noticed a group of people leave one of the elevators. He saw his parents in this group and they were dressed in their finest. They looked particularly prosperous. Then, he saw the Davenports with a hotel employee pushing George in his wheelchair through the crowd. Don's eyes focused on a beauty in a mink coat just behind them.

That can't be Celia, can it? He moved quickly to catch up to her when a group of boisterous revelers pushed in front of him. Don swore to himself and tried to shove this group aside, but there were too many of them. He called out to his parents over the crowd noise, but his voice was lost in the din.

When he finally pushed through the group of partygoers, he caught up with his parents outside the elevator. They told their son that the Davenports and Celia had left, and that dinner had been canceled. Don was crestfallen.

CHAPTER SIX – MICHAEL GREEN

Fifth Avenue, Upper East Side

Michael Green sat quietly in front of the bay window in his brownstone living room reading *The New York Times*. Dressed casually in his undershirt, he had a view of the street and the front walk-up. He was about to enjoy a coffee and roll that the cook had brought in when his neighbors walked past. He suddenly pushed the cook aside to wave at them, but they could not see him through the white lace curtains. Disconcerted, Michael shouted at his neighbors, but they could not hear him through all the outside street noise. He considered running out into the street but got a glimpse of his undershirt and uncombed hair in the mirror and sat back down. Then, Michael rationalized that running out after the Davenports so he could talk to their niece, Celia, was unbecoming, just as it was inappropriate.

Even so, Celia had become really quite something now. She was ravishing. Overnight, it seemed, she had transformed into a woman.

His mother walked into the living room where she found Michael with his nose to the windowpane. She looked out to discover what was so interesting. Then, she smiled and turned to her son,

"I see that their little girl has grown up. What would you say if I invited our neighbors and Celia to Sunday lunch?"

CHAPTER SEVEN – THE GODFATHER

Upper West Side, New York City

The car dealership was located at 96th Avenue West and Amsterdam. It was far enough from the Upper East Side to fetch a cheap rent, and close enough to attract rich buyers of all sorts of cars.

A used car salesman in the dealership was certain that a high roller had just driven up with his driver. It was the hat that gave the high roller away. While the driver wore only a fashionable but worn flat cap, the older man sitting in the back seat donned a navy-blue Fedora with a white-striped satin ribbon.

With his narrow face, sideburns, and near-set eagle eyes of a bright yellow, the salesman resembled a large, balding bird of prey. Or was it Vincent Van Gogh resuscitated? In any event, the salesman immediately spotted the one with the high net worth, but why was this gentleman in the Fedora seated in the back seat? The salesman rushed out to meet his prey before anyone else could and waved at them to follow him over to the side where the new 1917 models were parked.

At this point, one of his colleagues walked up to take the sale, but Bill Rett—that was the car salesman's name—shooed him away,

"Beat it, Johnny, I got these guys."

The two potential buyers pulled over and stopped. Bill Rett tried to open the back door of their Oldsmobile, but it was locked. The driver, James Metz, who had jumped out upon arrival, just stared at the used car salesman with his hand already on the door handle. So did the passenger in the back.

Rett removed his hand and smiled, "May I help you gentlemen?"

He was greeted with more silence, but began his spiel anyway, "I see you're driving a 1915 Olds, but I got something much better." He banged on the hood of a car right next to him. "I can offer you gentlemen this wonderful 1917 sedan whose Model T father was priced at $850 in 1909, but now it's going for a measly $360. People talk about prices going up all the time but not so here! Anyway, this one's got a ladder chassis, an inline four-cylinder, 2.9-liter cast iron block, side valves, a three-bearing crankshaft with splash lubrication, the whole churning out twenty horsepower. Just imagine twenty racehorses pulling you along."

Rett had addressed this whole dialogue to the older man in the backseat and had ignored the driver entirely. He noticed the old man's legs were frail and linked together, and there was a wheelchair next to him.

Unfortunately, the sun appeared so Rett had to peer up at the cripple and wait for him to say something. But the old man didn't oblige. The silence was deafening until the elder nodded his head slightly at his driver/mechanic.

Metz walked over to the cabin of the Tudor Saloon and said, "No gas pedal?"

"No. Instead, it has throttle and ignition timing lines on the steering wheel," said Rett. "Epicyclic gears. Two forward speeds plus reverse and neutral. High and low gears selected using the left-hand pedal. Middle pedal for reverse. And there's the right-hand pedal for a transmission brake."

The salesman looked at both customers searching for signs. There were none from the old man. The driver said nothing and crawled under the car. Then, he called out, "Both axles on transverse leaf springs. There's excellent ground clearance for farms." But there was no reaction from the old man, his employer, so the driver crawled out from under and opened the side door of the car.

"Do you want a two- or four-seater?" said Rett.

There was still no answer as the driver walked to the front of the car and opened the hood. The used-car salesman kept talking, "Bore and stroke 85x101, Holley carburetors, twenty horsepower at 1800 rpm. Wood spoke wheels, mechanical brakes on rear wheels only. Maximum speed, 42 mph."

Bill Rett studied both men again before completing his pitch, "Mr. Ford makes one of these Model T's every ninety minutes." He pointed to his watch for emphasis. This was normally the climax of his speech, but the reaction of these men was different.

The old man studied Rett for ten seconds before he finally turned to the driver and said, "Metz, make sure you can lift me into the rear seat."

"Yes, sir," said Metz. The old man unlocked the back door. Metz went in and carried his employer out and into the rear seat of the new Model T. Then, Metz fetched the wheelchair and placed it in there as well. The fit was perfect. Only then did the old man address the used-car salesman,

"Thank you. Payment will be arranged for three cars, and you may deliver them to my Fifth Avenue address."

Bill Rett was astonished. He was about to say something when the old man cut him off and said, "Metz, I will leave the inspection and purchase of the Cadillac and Rolls Royce in your hands."

CHAPTER EIGHT – THE INVITATION

Fifth Avenue, Upper East Side

Betty Davenport wheeled her husband across the expansive living room to the liquor cabinet, which had been lowered and equipped to handle his special needs. He loved to drop a couple of large cubes of ice and a double-shot of Jack Daniels into one of his smoked-glass, monogrammed tumblers. Then, he'd open a small tin of cashews, tilt his chair back, and gaze out through the curtains onto the busy street.

There was a noise at the letter box, and Betty walked over to the front door. There on top of a stack of mail was a white envelope decorated with red flowers. It was from Ruth Green. Betty opened the envelope immediately, being careful not to tear the contents. She thought of her chance meeting the other day with Ruth over at Bergdorf's as she unfolded the letter.

"Dear Mr. and Mrs. Davenport, it was wonderful meeting you the other day over at Bergdorf Goodman.

We're having a sendoff party in honor of Michael, and his ..." Betty skipped to the important part.

"George, darling, we've been invited to a party at the Green's house. You know the Greens, don't you?"

"Of course, Betty."

"You know, her husband Lloyd Green is a senior partner at the Wall Street bank, Steiner Carlton Green, don't you?"

"Yes, of course, dear, I know him."

"Well? Should we accept? I hear they have wonderful entertainment at their parties. They often invite an opera singer or a famous pianist to perform for the other guests."

George Davenport had started twirling his Jack Daniels as soon as he heard the word 'invited'. He wanted to stall for time before he answered Betty. The Steiners were lovely people, except when they touted that Austrian bank of theirs, which was most of the time. And Lloyd Green had been a bit of a roughneck when he was young. George often referred to Lloyd as the 'horse-riding banker.'

"Oh Betty, you know how I dislike having to attend these events. Everyone spends so much time standing around, while I, I..." George looked down at his wheelchair."

"Oh George..." Betty stopped as she remembered how handsome, strong, and athletic her husband used to be. While Lloyd Green rode the range on his horse,

George Davenport rode buffaloes to 'relax,' as he put it. And when he wasn't relaxing, he was building a railroad empire out west. It saddened Betty to think her husband was now forced to sit in a chair all the time.

"No, I won't be going," George said. "Besides, Lloyd is always touting his bank and looking for business. That's what their kind usually do. I prefer to remain with J.P. Morgan."

"I'm sorry, dear, you feel that way. But what do we do about Celia? She was included in the invitation, and I'm sure she would want to go."

"Of course, Betty, don't let me put a dampener on your fun. Bring her, for sure, if she wants to."

JAYNE LOUISE CRAMFORDE AND RICHARD BONTE

CHAPTER NINE – THE HIRED HAND

"Where shall we go, Auntie?" said Celia, standing tall and erect on the porch of their Fifth Avenue mansion. Dressed in a pink silk blouse, brown flared skirt, and matching tailored jacket, Celia made quite a picture with her Aunt Betty, who wore a white linen flared skirt and raised hemline. They wore matching broad-brimmed hats with ribbons for Celia and pink artificial flowers for Betty. Men in passing cabs and seated on horse-drawn carriages looked on appreciatively as the dynamic duo walked out onto the sidewalk.

"You mean, *how* shall we go?" said Betty.

"Oh, let's take the new car, it's so beautiful."

"I know, dear, but those automobiles are so noisy and brash. And we're right on the street. We can easily hail a horse and carriage." With that, she raised her arm and a horse-drawn taxi pulled over for them. Celia waved it off. She tugged on her aunt's sleeve.

"Come on, Auntie, let's go round the back and get the driver to take us to Lord and Taylor."

Aunt Betty allowed her impetuous niece to lead her to the back garage where the three cars that George Davenport had just bought were sitting. However, the aunt and niece didn't expect to see James Metz, the hired hand, stripped to the waist and sweating over a carburetor spraying gas over the motor.

"Oh dear," said Betty, and she instinctively covered her niece's eyes, "Please excuse us."

James Metz's large biceps flexed as he manipulated an enormous wrench to shut off the defective carburetor. He jumped in surprise as Celia angrily ripped her aunt's hand away. "I'm eighteen, now, Auntie!" she hissed.

"Sorry, Ladies," said Metz, wiping off with a soiled towel. "The carb was sprayin' oil. I didn't want to get dirty."

Betty chuckled, "Looks like you're a little late there."

Celia, however, just stared at the male specimen in front of her. He was not afraid to return the young lady's stare and took his time as he wiped down and grabbed his shirt. Then, he slung it casually over his back and head. Celia was conscious of the perfect "V" his waist formed with his shoulders, as he slowly buttoned up his shirt. He seemed neither embarrassed by the interruption nor the attention and wore an insolent smile on his lips. *My God, he's just the hired help. What will I do?* thought Celia.

Betty and Celia turned back to the street to hail a horse and carriage. Celia noticed that she was now perspiring and had flushed bright red.

JAYNE LOUISE CRAMFORDE AND RICHARD BONTE

CHAPTER TEN – THE FOOTBALL STAR

Central Park, New York City

Ever since he had seen her leave the Plaza after his arrival from Chicago, Don Casterson wanted to know more. He wanted to know everything about Celia Dawes, and why she was staying with her aunt and uncle. He could not believe how she had changed from when she was fifteen to the mature, gorgeous woman he had glimpsed from afar in the Plaza lobby that day.

He lengthened his strides on this perfect spring day to cover more ground and arrive at least fifteen minutes ahead of time. The luncheon was set for one o'clock, but Don wanted to look around and find the perfect place for them to sit in the hotel dining room. Although he was only twenty-five and not completely established in business, Don had decided he would invite his parents, the Davenports, and their niece to lunch. He was what they call in business, 'being proactive.' Even though he had been invited by the Davenports, he wanted to manage the meeting. It was important for Don to be in charge, and not dependent on his parents. George Davenport would respect him for that, and even more importantly, so would Celia.

He swung his arms back and forth vigorously as he walked along the winding paths of Central Park. From time to time, when he wasn't looking down to sidestep horse dung, he would dodge an out-of-control calash or larger horse and carriage. He would shake his head or clench his teeth and thrust his jaw out. He thought back to his days in Chicago when he was a high school football star and was even considered a prospect for the high-powered *Decatur Staleys* Football Club. And then he went to Yale and became *that* college star, *the* Yale quarterback. This top-level experience finally made Don realize that Chicago was provincial, and of little interest on the world stage. The Eastern Seaboard was where it was at, and particularly New York City. He had decided that Manhattan was where he was going to make a start in life.

He noticed the sprinkling of light green the bare winter branches had taken on during the first few days of spring. Soon there would be blankets of white and yellow camelias, along with tulips inhabiting these beds of lush green. He brushed aside these errant poetic thoughts as he considered a fork in the path. It was not hard to choose which way to go as the sunlit-bathed Plaza and the gilded "P" letters on its heart-shaped crest came into view in the distance. Don swung his spring coat over his shoulder and walked another half-mile. He finally entered the Plaza.

He made his way over to the dining room and allowed the maître d' to show him his table. Don was very serious when he talked to people from the lower classes. He often moved too close to them and jutted his large chin out, so he appeared to be looking down at them, which he was.

Only five minutes later, the Davenports arrived. George Davenport was wheeled in by Metz along with Mrs. Davenport and Celia. Don made a big show of tipping the maître d' as Metz wheeled George Davenport to the table first. Don approached a bit too close, and almost knocked into Metz as the driver tried to draw out Betty's seat for her. The two men looked at each other briefly, whereupon Metz walked off to wait for his employers outside in the Rolls Royce. Don smiled at Celia whose eyes were following Metz.

As Don now pulled out Celia's chair for her, Betty Davenport made a delicate ballet-like gesture with her hand and said to her niece, "Celia, do you remember Mr. Casterson?"

Then, she nodded at Don and smiled, but Don said, "Well, I remember you, Celia, when you were just sweet sixteen—"

"And never been kissed?" Celia shot out.

47

"Celia!" Mrs. Davenport, "how rude of you!" Uncle George glared at his niece and then called for the wine list.

"I don't think so, Mrs. Davenport, if you don't mind my saying," said Don as he looked lovingly at Celia.

Celia, who had been looking at everything and anybody except Don, now looked him full in the eyes and said, "So, Mr. Casterson, what brings you to New York?"

"Please, call me 'Don,'" said Don.

"Alright then, 'Don,'" said Celia with a big smile, "What brings you to New York?"

CHAPTER ELEVEN – THE PARTY

Fifth Avenue, Upper East Side

The muffled sounds of clarinets, oboes, and trombones could be heard as the driver, Metz, pulled up in front of the Green residence on Fifth Avenue. The Greens and Davenports were only ten blocks removed from each other, but tonight they were a world apart. Betty Davenport had left the wheelchair-bound George in the care of the housekeeper so she could become young again in the company of her beautiful niece.

Metz jumped out, ran around the Rolls Royce, and extended his hand to Betty. She was wearing a Paul Poiret grey satin evening gown over silk stockings and a wide-brimmed hat.

Then, he helped Celia alight. She was beautiful in her light blue chiffon silk, matching stockings, and smart black shoes. Celia leaned more than necessary on Metz' arm as she purposely lost her balance and pushed into him.

"Thank you, Metz. Could you return in three hours to pick us up?" said Betty.

"Yes, Ma'am," said Metz, still holding onto an apparently unsteady Celia. "Are you ok, Miss Dawes?"

"I'll be fine. Thank you, Metz."

When they were out of earshot, Celia whispered to Betty, "Auntie, do you think Metz knows how to dance? He had such a firm grip on me."

"Celia, I'm sure he does, but you'll find much better game inside."

Betty Davenport loved having her niece stay with her. Poor George was wheelchair-bound, and although Betty loved him dearly, she couldn't get enough of Celia's chatter, her feelings, her worries, and everything a young girl of eighteen would be concerned about. Celia's adolescence was Betty's youth all over again. Right now—and for both—nothing was more important than the Greens' party.

"I love big parties, don't you, Auntie?" said Celia. "You can get lost in them and meet all sorts of people. Small parties are boring. I feel like I'm under a microscope."

A blast of noise greeted the aunt and niece as the front door opened. Six musicians were blowing into various horns in front of a bassist and a drummer, as thirty couples in evening wear foxtrotted around the room. Two dozen more people smoked and talked animatedly at small tables pushed off to the side in the high-ceilinged area.

"Hello, Mrs. Davenport. Hello, Celia, so glad you could come," Ruth Green shouted above the noise. "You're both looking beautiful. As you can see, I'm dressed in green, like my name." Mrs. Green wore a green satin evening gown, matching hat, and stockings with fashionable, low-heeled black pumps.

Different colored beads and streamers hung from the rafters. Waiters and other hired help walked quickly back and forth from the kitchen, and out to a vast outside garden that was also packed with revelers.

"Auntie, we came too late," said Celia.

"Never too late for a beautiful girl like you," said Betty. "I have learned from parties that one should arrive late and leave early. Always leave them wanting more."

"Are you saying we're going to be like Cinderella, Auntie?"

"Did you say 'Cinderella?'" Mrs. Green asked, as she seized both Celia and a frail, but good-looking young man, who was wandering about aimlessly.

"Excuse me, Mrs. Davenport. Let me borrow your niece for a bit." Mrs. Green nodded knowingly at Betty, like a yenta at a Jewish wedding, and said, "Celia, meet a young man with great potential. I am certain that one day he will be famous."

"Francis Fitzwilton," she said to the young man, "this is my neighbor's niece, Miss Celia Dawes." Mrs.

Green released her grip, so they could shake hands. As soon as they were alone, Celia said,

"Tell me, Mr. Fitzwilton, what will you be famous for?"

"Famous?"

"Yes, that's what Mrs. Green said." The music reached a crescendo here, almost drowning out Celia's words, but giving Mr. Fitzwilton a moment to reflect, so he said,

"Well, I hope she is referring to my desire and intention to be a successful novelist. Although, at the moment, that seems somewhat unlikely as my first full-length novel of 120,000 words has been rejected by Schriber's, you know, the publishers?"

"Oh, I'm sorry to hear that," said Celia. "Are you going to write another?"

"No, I've enlisted and am due to report to Leavenworth for officer training under Captain Dwight Eisenhower."

"Oh of course, that's so important for our country, but please, Mr. Fitzwilton, don't give up on your dream." Celia was very compassionate and eager to provide encouragement, so she said, "Tell me, how do you decide what to write about, and what your characters are like?"

"As far as characters are concerned," said the young writer above the din, "I study people and incorporate aspects of them into my fictional characters."

"Oh, Mr. Fitzwilton, that is so exciting."

"Really?"

"Yes. Will you incorporate me into one of your books?"

"Well, now that you mention it," said the writer, "you do remind me of a love once known and now lost."

"What was her name?" said Celia.

"Genevieve. I knew her in Chicago."

"Oh please, Mr. Fitzwilton, please keep writing. May I call you by your first name, Francis?"

"Well, actually, I don't really like that name and prefer my middle name, which is—"

The music drowned out his answer. Mrs. Green, who had been looking for her own son the whole time Mr. Fitzwilton was talking, suddenly whisked Celia away to present her to Michael.

"May I take her off your hands, mother?" said Michael Green, who had spotted Celia from across the room and had finally succeeded in pushing through the entire group to get to her.

"Why certainly, son, take her away, my good man," said Betty, who was standing nearby and had overheard.

"How about me? I'm Mr. Green, Senior," said Lloyd Green, who had swooped in like a bird of prey around Betty and her niece. "May I have this dance, Mrs. Davenport?"

"You don't mind if I dance with your husband, do you, Mrs. Green?" said Betty.

"Of course not, go ahead, Mrs. Davenport."

Betty acknowledged Ruth Green with a smile and nodded at Lloyd Green. "So gallant we are in the Green family," she said.

"Like son, like father," said Lloyd Green with a smile. And with that, the two couples inserted themselves into the revolving foxtrotting couples.

"I thought you might want to see me?" said Michael to Celia when they were alone.

"Oh no, Mr. Green, you thought wrong. I was kidnapped," she joked. Her beautiful smile belied her words as they began to dance. Michael's arms made a perfect frame as he held her firm against him. Dressed in his black tails, and with his dark hair parted down the middle, he was very handsome. Celia folded into him as they glided around the room.

"Call me Michael, Celia," said Michael Green. "Sorry, I didn't want to take you away from your date over there." He glanced quickly at Mr. Fitzwilton who was looking at them with envy. Celia acknowledged Mr. Fitzwilton with a wave and a big smile, but then returned her attention to Michael.

"He's not my *date*," said Celia.

"Sorry. Or your chaperone?" said Michael, motioning to Betty.

"You're not sorry, are you? Sounds like you came with your own chaperone as well?" said Celia, nodding at Lloyd Green, who was smoothly foxtrotting round the room with Betty.

"Except he does live here," said Michael, whirling Celia closer to her aunt and Lloyd Green.

"Easy, Michael, we don't want to get too close to our chaperones, do we now?" said Celia.

Still foxtrotting, Michael guided Celia into a seat near the back by the garden, and far from the others. The day had been cold, but the night was unseasonably warm, and a gust of wind through the open door ruffled the curtains and the streamers.

There was a break in the music, and Michael offered Celia a cigarette.

"No thanks, I don't smoke," she said.

Michael put his pack of cigarettes back in his pocket.

"Not to worry. I don't either. I just carry them around and offer them up to be social. You're spiky, you know that?" said Michael.

"What's that?" Celia said.

"You. You're spiky, and I like that," Michael repeated. "Care for a little walk outside in the garden and we can talk about it?" he added.

"You're smooth, Mr. Green, almost too smooth, but I like that," said Celia. "And I'd love to take a walk in the garden with you." *Everything is so easy with this fellow,* Celia thought.

The band started up again, but they forewent dancing and walked outside in the garden. Different colored gusts of wind picked up twirls of white smoke to follow them out. At the other end of the garden was another couple holding hands and looking into each other's eyes. Celia and Michael strolled for a bit, gazing at the heavens partially lit by the lights from inside. She looked up at Michael who reached out and held her hand. It was as if they had known each other for years.

"You still think I'm spiky?" she said.

CHAPTER TWELVE –YALE CREW

New London, Connecticut

He picked her up at New London Union Station in a bright yellow 1917 Dodge Roadster. He parked it right in front of this red brick building that looked like a huge barn. She had taken the 8:03 am train from New York, bringing her in at 11:37, right on time. He saw her step daintily off the train, and he was entranced. She was a vision of beauty, clothed in Coco Chanel silk underneath a large-brimmed white hat and parasol. She held her hand out to him, which he kissed, whereupon they made their way over to his two-seater roadster. Wearing a black wool Fedora and yellow vest that matched the color of his car, he was quite the man about town.

Betty Davenport had been a real sport in allowing her niece to go unchaperoned to New London to meet Don Casterson. Celia had promised Aunt Betty to take the return train back to New York at 6:07 pm and return approximately three and a half hours later at 9:30 pm that night. Betty assumed her precocious niece would abide by the rules of decency during the afternoon, and that Don would be the model gentleman. After all, there was no reason to assume otherwise. He was to bring her to the Harvard/Yale Regatta and watch Yale's Bulldogs crew team take on the Crimson. Except that when they drove up to the start of the race, they discovered that, exceptionally this year, there would be no regatta. However—some passerby told them—if they really wanted to watch rowing, they could go to the Gilder Boathouse on the bank of the Housatonic River and observe the crew team practice from there.

'Practice?' Don had come to watch the Harvard/Yale Regatta, not some meaningless practice. Don was very annoyed about this. He was especially annoyed with himself. He should have checked to see if there was a race to begin with. The Regatta had started in the 1850s and had happened every year since then. It was a fixture of life at both Yale and Harvard. But just this year, 1917, they had cancelled it; *they* had cancelled his chance to impress an eighteen-year-old socialite from Manhattan. *Someone* had ruined Don's plan to impress Celia Dawes.

Don reasoned that Celia Dawes would not have made the long train trip up to New London if she weren't interested in, and very attracted to, him. He was not wrong. And, except for this one crucial detail, Don had planned their day perfectly. An ex-quarterback on the football team—an ex-star—Don Casterson was Yale Royalty. If the USA had had a Royal Family, he would have been one of its princes, possibly the king. It happened to be that at Yale, Don had an impeccable reputation. Accordingly, Don worked out that he would meet Celia, impress her with his new Roadster, take her to the Regatta, and then show her his hotel room. And all by 4:00 pm so she could make her 6:07 pm return train ride. But because of some silly scheduling problem, his plan had failed. What was he to do?

He didn't have to do too much. He just had to *be* and let his bigger-than-life personality shine through. Celia was more than impressed. From the Housatonic River, they strolled along the New London Thames where the Regatta normally took place. With reams and reams of words, Don brought to life past regattas he had seen, even pointing at the water where a Yale canoe had once raced past the Harvard one in the 1914 race. In fact, Yale had won in '14 and '15 by twenty seconds only to 'blow' it in '16 when Harvard won.

Then, they walked through the ivy-colored brick buildings and over to the football field where Don had had so much success. Don regaled her with sports war stories over lunch, and more stories about himself over tea. They held hands and gazed into each other's eyes, strolled again through ivy-colored walls, and drove through New London in his roadster. When it was close to six pm, and they finally arrived back at Union Station so Celia could return to New York, she was in love and thought that Don would be the perfect marriage partner.

As she climbed into the train, she turned back to blow Don a kiss. Don was all smiles as he returned her kiss, but secretly, he regretted not fulfilling his carnal desire for her. It had always been Don's plan to bring her to his hotel room for an afternoon romp. In his all or nothing, win/lose mentality, he felt he had lost this battle. However, Celia was over the moon about him.

Ironically, Don Casterson had won the war.

CHAPTER THIRTEEN – GREEN CARLTON STEINER

Central Park, New York City

The Model T Ford screamed around the hairpin turn on two wheels but landed back on four after Michael Green completed his maneuver. Celia screamed and clutched him in fright. They had almost capsized into Turtle Pond. He came to a sudden stop and grabbed her so she wouldn't plunge forward. She screamed again and started beating on him. "What's the matter with you? You could have killed us both there."

"Naaahhh," said Michael. Then, he started laughing hysterically and removed her little fists as if they were toothpicks, placing them in her lap. Nonplussed, Celia stared at him.

"I thought you were more serious," Celia said. "Boy, was I mistaken."

"Oh, come on, Celia, I've done this turn dozens of times before. I knew I was going out with you, so I've been practicing."

"Great! So, I'm your guinea pig now?"

"Come on, Celia, lighten up. Let's drive downtown. It'll only be about ten to fifteen minutes."

"Why downtown, Michael? There's nothing of interest there."

"I don't know, Celia. I just find it fascinating. Where our wonderful New York began. I'll show you the old buildings and tell you what people did in them in the past."

I know what people did in old buildings, Michael, and I know what they're doing in new buildings. What's the matter with you? Don't you want to spend the afternoon with me at the Waldorf?

"Sure, Michael, why not, but I can only do such a trip if we have a party on the way. You know? If we have enough booze?"

"Certainly, Celia, of course." Although Celia was only a year younger than he, she seemed far more worldly, even if less mature. And Michael always had problems in these types of situations. Michael did not drink. At least not in the daytime. But he was a gentleman, so he stopped at a bar and bought a small bottle of white wine for Celia.

Being careful not to scare her anymore, Michael drove south into downtown Manhattan with care. As they sipped their drinks, Michael kept up a running commentary about different points of interest along the way. Meanwhile, Celia purred with delight, removed her hat, and let the wind remodel her curls.

Michael stopped the car to allow a well-dressed young woman to cross the road to a waiting tram car. "Number 195, Broadway, AT&T," he said excitedly, pointing to the tram. Then, he indicated a twenty-one-story building across from the tramway line. Celia nodded absently without looking at the building. She seemed to be only interested in the coat the woman was wearing.

He continued driving south along Broadway and at number 120, he pointed to the forty-one-story building there.

"This building's just four years old. The Equitable Insurance headquarters. All the major insurance companies are here."

Celia grunted and took another sip of her drink. At number 71, Michael tried again to interest her in the sights of New York. He pointed to an eighteen-story building. "One of the oldest skyscrapers in New York. US Steel, built, I think, in 1895." Celia said nothing as she rummaged in her bag for something.

At number 65, Michel pointed to a new twenty-one-story building. "American Express," he said. There was still no reaction from Celia.

Michael stopped the car for a moment. He realized he was in danger of appearing to be a complete bore, so he decided on one last try. He made a U-turn and headed back north along Broadway. At number 233, he slammed on the brakes. Celia spilt her drink.

"Look at this one built in 1911. The Woolworth building, fifty-one stories high. The tallest skyscraper in New York, and possibly the world. They say you could never build anything taller."

Celia was not impressed, "You mean the Five and Dime building? I never shop there."

Michael then turned the car south and headed for Wall Street. He gave it yet another try at number 26 Broadway.

"Standard Oil, thirty-one stories high?" but his voice sounded defeated. Suddenly, Celia noticed the next building at number 25 and shouted with joy, "Cunard!"

Michael became animated again, "Yes, Celia, a brand-new thirty-five floors. All the major shipping companies are here. They call it Steamship Row."

"Well, Michael, I don't care how tall their office buildings are. I only care how luxurious their ships are. I want to make a trip on one to France and see Paris."

"I don't think that would be a good idea this year, Celia. There are German submarines lurking in the North Atlantic and France is at war."

"Oh, I forgot about that horrible war in Europe." Celia took another sip of what was left of her Chardonnay.

At last, he parked his Model T on Wall Street and pointed to a high-rise office building. "That's my father's firm. Among many other things, they invest in, and back, the booming new business of cinema."

"*Green Carlton Steiner?* So, you are the *Green*? The first in the company name. Is that important?" said Celia.

"No, of course not," said Michael. It is a partnership of the Greens here in New York, the Carlton Smythes in London, and the Steiners in Berlin."

"Oh, so you're aligned with Germans?" said Celia, and Michael could hear the disappointment in her voice. He was not wrong.

Celia hesitated whether to bring the horrible war that was raging in Europe into the conversation. She decided against it, so she said, "Can we go in and meet your father?"

"I'm sorry, Celia, I don't believe he will appreciate having his work interrupted."

"Oh please, Michael, let's give it a try."

Michael looked at Celia with annoyance. She was a problem because she always took him out of his comfort zone, but she was so beautiful that he was ready to go against his principles to satisfy her.

"Follow me," he said. He knocked on, and held open, the imposing oak doors and followed her inside.

"Specially imported from England," he mentioned, to see her reaction. But there was none, so he gave his name to the receptionist who then smiled and pointed to the elevators,

"Eleventh floor," she said. They entered the elevator carriage with two other people. The operator held the control wheel to ensure none of the passengers could touch it and interfere with the operation.

After a first stop, the metal concertina doors opened on the eleventh floor. It was sunny and bright, and Michael and Celia made their way to another large oak door featuring a discreet white plaque with embossed green letters, "Green Carlton Steiner." A short, sickly, and rheumatic young man of eighteen was seated behind a big desk with the name, "Irving Thalberg," written on it. He was making notes from a heavy law book opened on his desk.

"Hello, Irving," said Michael, "How are you?"

"Fine, thank you, Mr. Green."

"Have you seen my father?"

"He stepped out. I believe he'll be gone for the rest of the day."

"Oh, that's too bad. Celia, this is Irving Thalberg. He is working temporarily here at the bank on our cinematic and motion picture interests. I believe one day he will be a very important person."

Celia held out her hand to the young man, "How do you do, Mr. Thalberg? I hope you will remember me when you're famous."

Irving Thalberg gave her a genuine, but closed-lip smile, "I could never forget such a beautiful lady, Miss Celia."

JAYNE LOUISE CRAMFORDE AND RICHARD BONTE

CHAPTER FOURTEEN - THE METROPOLITAN

1411 Broadway at 39th Street

"Don, don't you just love this place?" Celia gushed. The seats at the Metropolitan were of red plush velour, the ceiling was immense, and everyone was dressed in the finest evening wear. Don and Celia's seats were the best in the house, just three rows up, and plumb center.

Today, Celia found herself with yet another suitor, posing as a tour guide. When it came to knowledge and culture, Don Casterson, despite his six-year-age advantage, was far behind Michael Green.

"Yes, it is magnificent, Celia," said Don. "And I happen to know something about its history," he added.

"I don't believe you, Don. I never imagined you to be an opera patron."

Don was inwardly ecstatic. This was his opportunity to fool Celia. Don had made a special effort the week earlier to visit the Metropolitan and familiarize himself with its layout so he could appear to be a regular visitor. He smiled, puffed out his chest and said, "Celia, I bet you didn't know the Metropolitan was inaugurated with a performance of Faust in 1883?"

"Actually, Don, I did know that." Celia laughed.

"Right, Celia, but do you really know who designed it?"

"No Don, I have no idea," she smiled, but she smelled a rat. "Pray tell."

"It was a fellow called Cody."

Celia now knew she had Don. She smiled and let him wait before she pierced his balloon, "No, it wasn't, silly. You're mixing him up with Wild Bill Cody. It was a man named J. Cleaveland Cady. See, "Cady" is spelled with an "a" not an "o.""

Don was so crestfallen that Celia laughed and squeezed his arm affectionately, and whispered, "It was so wonderful of you to make such an effort to try and impress me." Her smile was genuine, so Don relaxed,

"Oh well," he said, "I suppose I better stick to polo."

"Yes, Don, you're better at that, but be quiet now, the performance is about to start."

CHAPTER FIFTEEN – GERI SOUTHERN

West Side Tennis Club, Forest Hills, New York

Alternatively looking from the hoop ahead to the croquet ball directly below her, practiced golfer Geri Southern, 16, was hunched over in concentration. Even if it was not golf, every sport deserved the same attention. Geri wore her hair short, as was the fashion, and she was good-looking in an androgynous way. She was tall and bony, and wore a brassiere, although she did not need one. She also had on a blue sports corset she'd seen in a magazine ad for 'sports and dancing,' although she didn't need it. It had always been her intention to become a professional golfer.

Leaning on her croquet club, Celia stared with admiration at her younger friend. She had witnessed Geri many times in the same position hunched over a putter. How could Geri remain so concentrated over silly games like croquet, golf, or tennis?

Geri kept weighing up the shot she was about to make, always looking from the ball to the hoop and the wicket beyond.

"Geri, have you ever imagined being a boy?" Celia asked.

"A boy, Celia?" This question broke Geri's concentration, and she looked up at her older friend.

"Yes, well after all, you are a super golfer," said Celia. Probably as good as any of the men. Isn't that true?"

Geri considered this and smiled, "Well, thank you for the compliment."

"I can't imagine ever wanting to be a boy. But what about you, Geri? Even your name could go both ways. And you are tall for a girl. You have more muscles than I do—even though you are two years younger—but far smaller breasts."

As she ran her hands along her breasts and undulated her hips slightly, Celia held in her stomach and pulled her shoulders back. The difference in body shape and femininity between the two was startling. Geri smiled as if the matter was of no concern or importance to her and returned to her croquet mallet.

"I could teach you to golf, Celia."

"Oh Geri, you know I'd be useless. Let's not kid ourselves."

Geri said nothing as she concentrated on hitting the ball. She tapped it perfectly, straight through to the wicket, and without touching either side of the hoop.

JAYNE LOUISE CRAMFORDE AND RICHARD BONTE

CHAPTER SIXTEEN – MANUAL ASSISTANCE

Davenport Residence – Fifth Avenue, Upper East Side

It was a cold and sunny spring day, but Celia Dawes felt very warm.

"Metz, please help me up."

"Certainly, Miss Celia." Metz held out his hand to steady Celia as she climbed into the back seat of the car. His hand was massive, rough, and cold while hers was dainty, smooth, and hot, almost feverish to the touch. She left her hand in his before he finally released it and walked to resume his place behind the wheel.

She sat down delicately and leaned way back. She was afraid to sit on the edge of her seat and give in to her fitful thoughts that wanted nothing better for her body than to thrust forward and twist upwards like a tornado, only to encircle and squeeze to death the man in front of her. "Oh no, no," left her lips.

Metz turned back to find Celia staring at him, her eyes glistening with heat and desire, "Pardon, Miss Celia, did you say something?"

"What?" Celia flushed an even deeper shade of red, almost scarlet, as she realized her innermost thoughts had left her lips. "Oh no, nothing, Metz."

"Where to, Miss Celia?"

Celia didn't know where she wanted to go. She could feel the hard seat beneath her corset and just wanted to fall back in bed, but she chased that thought from her mind and said, "Let's go for a drive around Central Park."

"Sure thing, Miss Celia."

Embarrassed, Celia tried to think 'cold thoughts' as she bounced about on the back seat, the hard springs of which egged on her torrid fantasies. She stared through the window at the specks of green buds on the trees and the meager remnants of snow outside. She wanted to keep her eyes fixed on anything, or anybody, but the driver seated in the front seat.

They drove in silence for about fifteen minutes. Holding his massive forearms straight on the wheel at the ten and two positions, Metz would glance in the rearview mirror from time to time to see if Miss Celia was alright. He sensed there was something wrong with her, but she only stared through the window.

"Tell me something about yourself, Metz," she finally said. In surprise, Metz glanced up in the mirror to find her sitting forward in her seat, and with her eyes glued to his in the mirror. He immediately looked straight ahead and thought about what he could possibly say to her. Would he say the right thing? Should he tell her some lies? What about the five years he had spent on the yacht with Cody, or the slum he now lived in? He glanced up again to field a slew of questions directed at him.

"Do you have a girlfriend, Metz? Is she pretty? Does she have dark hair, or is she fair-haired like me? Is she fat? No, you wouldn't have a fat girlfriend. Can she cook? I expect she can cook."

Before he could reply, he felt the soft caress of Celia's hand on the back of his neck, and then it stopped. Had he imagined it?...

JAYNE LOUISE CRAMFORDE AND RICHARD BONTE

CHAPTER SEVENTEEN – LOOKERS

Lookers Restaurant, Broadway and 59th St., New York City

Mostly young, ex-Yale men now residing in New York City had gathered at Lookers Restaurant at Broadway and 59th on the west side. It was the spring version of their bi-annual lunch in this classic restaurant—all red brick outside, and brown wainscoted paneling inside—with a long bar in the front. There were twenty loud and opinionated ex-bulldogs assembled around a long, rectangular table. A shapely young barmaid was busy carrying drinks back and forth from the bar. Don Casterson was seated at the head of the table along with many star players from the so-called 'Gilded Age' Yale Football team of 1910-1914.

"Nonsense, Green, you people have no idea!" Don shouted at his younger cohort seated on the left so everyone could hear. Nineteen-year-old Michael was in awe of his new friend who was about six years his senior. That Michael had even managed an invitation to the closed-circle luncheon with these older men was partly due to his friendship with Don Casterson. Don was also friendly with the younger man because he might be a good contact if Don were ever to do business with or work for Green Carlton Steiner. Michael was the son of one of the founders. Even though Michael was five foot ten, he was slender and small compared to the other football stars around the table. In contrast, ex-quarterback Don Casterson towered above him, and had a booming voice to match his muscular appearance.

"All this so-called 'science'," Don said, "Science, be damned. What do they claim? Oh yes, that we all stem from apes, yeah right."

"No, Mr. Casterson, that's not quite right," Michael let out plaintively.

Don doubled down, "No? Green, even the suggestion that the human race began in Africa, even *that* suggestion, for God's sake, is ridiculous. Africa? Africa, of all places? Utter nonsense. If that were the case, we would all be black, wouldn't we? And as you can see ..."

Don pulled up his jacket and sleeve to reveal his forearm, "... Look carefully at the color of my skin—one of the forty shades of white, by the way—isn't that totally different from the black slaves of Georgia? Well, obviously they aren't slaves anymore, but you know what I mean?"

Don went silent for a moment because he felt embarrassed. He had become too emotional, especially since he believed himself to be both unemotional and logical. And he had become too loud. "Pardon me, Mr. Green, you say you are studying medicine?"

"Yes, Mr. Casterson."

"Well look, Green, as a future doctor, surely you must have some opinion on immigration? What I mean is, I have done a lot of study on this subject. And my question is, what on earth are we going to do about the growing slums of New York?"

Seeing that the others had gone silent and were listening to him, Don again raised his voice so that he could not only inform his table but other tables nearby, "There are hundreds of thousands of immigrants in New York. Back in 1900, we had 1.3 million foreign-born residents. At the rate they're coming in now, that number will reach two million by 1920. These people tend to stay where others of their kind have already settled. Look at Chinatown, Little Italy, and the Lower East Side. Just go down there and see how awful it is. These people are practically living on the streets. The streets are forty feet wide, but you'd never know it with all their horrible vendor carts lined up on each side. They're coming in at the rate of half a million a year from central, eastern, and southern Europe. The flotsam of the world!"

"Just a minute, Mr. Casterson, hold on," Michael tried to interrupt, "Wait a minute."

"No, Green, we can't wait. We need to build a wall. Yes, a giant wall around this wonderful country of ours. Otherwise, we'll be overrun and replaced."

"Mr. Casterson, please, I have to stop you there."

Don and everyone stared at Michael. *Oh God, what have I done now? Have I been too insulting? I'm a guest here. Maybe they won't have me back?*

Michael looked around the table and said, "I'm sorry. I didn't mean to be impolite, but if you will allow me to say a few words."

"Of course, Green, please, go ahead," said Don, who didn't want to admit he had previously monopolized the conversation.

"Alright then, thank you, Mr. Casterson." Michael cleared his throat and addressed the others as well. "Gentlemen, Mr. Casterson," he began in a small but tinny voice. "I'd just like to thank you for allowing me to attend your private gathering of Yale students past and present, and of course, the restaurant for providing such a great venue and wonderful food. Gentlemen, I can understand your hope and desire that something be done to improve the lot of the lower classes, especially those who are new to our great country. In fact, my mother is one of the charity workers who leaves her very expensive 5th Avenue home every day to help those far less fortunate than we are, and in any way she can, either by providing clothing or extra food to the people you have mentioned, but that is not the point I wanted to make."

"Look, Green, or whatever your name is," said another diner who had had too much to drink, "Yes, yes, your family is wonderful, we are wonderful, the restaurant is wonderful, but please, get on with it. What are you trying to say?"

"Boo-oo-ooo. Boo-oo-oo," went the other diners. "Let him speak."

"Sorry to be longwinded, thank you," Michael said. Then, he turned to Don. "Correct me if I am wrong, Mr. Casterson, but it seems to me you are assuming this rabble is going to remain the great unwashed forever?"

"Green," Don said. "You must see these people. Most can't even speak English. They prattle on in Italian, Russian, or Yiddish, or whatever. At least we Nordic types learned the language when we came here, if we weren't Scottish, English, Irish, or Welsh to begin with."

"Gentlemen," Michael said, "I accept that those who came to America in their forties or later are unlikely to assimilate easily, but, just like previous generations of immigrants, their children will become good Americans. Look at me, my forebears were partly from Germany."

Another Yale diner threw a roll and hit Michael in the head, "Goddamn Germans," he yelled, "Green, go back and live with those goddamn warmongers. Look what they're doing over there in France. We should be involved in this war, and I'm going to start with you, Green."

"Settle down," Don said to the offender. "Otherwise, we're going to be thrown out of here and banned from coming back, which will really piss me off."

He turned back to Michael and said, "So Green, what you're saying is that the offspring of these Bolsheviks in the lower east side are one day going to be my doctor, dentist, or lawyer, for Chrissake?"

And then the fellow that threw the roll yelled, "Yeah, right, sure thing. And one day, one of those black slaves' offspring is going to be president of the USA!"

With that, everyone broke into raucous laughter and toasted each other.

CHAPTER EIGHTEEN — GERI'S BROTHER

Barrington Hotel, Upper West Side, New York City

Geri Southern stepped out of the yellow cab at 81st and Columbus, paid the driver, and carried her large Louis Vuitton bag into the courtyard of the Barrington Hotel. She looked up at the imposing doorway set into the seven-story building of Roman brick and terra cotta that had only been built six years earlier in 1911. She took a long breath and let out a deep sigh. Then, she walked to the door that magically opened for her, nodded at the doorman, and walked to the hotel reception desk. A plain, middle-aged matron smiled at her, checked her in, and gave her the key to her room.

"My brother will probably be going out alone this evening," said Geri, before she left reception.

"Of course, Miss Southern. I'll tell the night clerk."

Once in her room, Geri quickly placed her clothes and toiletries away. Then, she lay on her bed and stared at the ceiling. *"Will I feel that same compulsion again tonight?"* she said to herself aloud. *"Go back to Wichita. Go home. You don't belong here."* Geri closed her eyes and began to weep. *"Why me? Why did it have to happen? What did I ever do to anybody to deserve this?"*

She frantically pulled at her sweater and observed her slightly enlarged cherries she deigned to call breasts. Then, she collapsed on her bed, and sobbed into the pillow. Tired and distraught, she fell asleep.

One hour later, she had recovered, and that wonderful thrill had come back to overtake her mind. She stripped off her clothes, showered, and drew a tattoo on the back of her left hand. She removed some theater make-up from her beauty case and went to work.

After fifteen minutes, she had the appearance she wanted. There was a dark shadow over the lower half of her face. She walked back into the bedroom and opened the closet doors. She avoided looking at the reflection of her naked body in the full-length mirror.

She examined each of the six suits she had brought. She chose the dark grey, double-breasted-with-chalked-stripes one. Then, she picked out a clean white shirt, blue-striped tie, matching hat, and brogue shoes, especially imported from England. She quickly put these items on, adjusted her tie, and looked at herself in the mirror.

"Perfect," she said aloud. *"This is the real me."*

Gone were the thoughts of returning to Wichita. *NYC is the place to be.* Here, Geri was not alone. There were others just like her in this wonderful metropolis. There would be others who would compliment her on her appearance. And bravery. *Yes, I'm brave.* Up to this point, she hadn't really appreciated the fact that she was indeed courageous.

She grinned, winked at herself, and left the room. She stood tall in the elevator and walked with a swagger by the reception desk.

The middle-aged female clerk from before smiled at her and said, "Good evening, Mr. Southern." Then, as Geri Southern strutted to the exit, the matron turned to the other clerk and whispered, "Good-looking guy. If only I was ten years younger ..."

JAYNE LOUISE CRAMFORDE AND RICHARD BONTE

CHAPTER NINETEEN – ROBBER BARONS

Fifth Avenue, Upper East Side

They were two of dozens of strollers taking in this warm Sunday afternoon on Fifth Avenue. Since it was not a workday, the traffic was less, but there still was a steady stream of horse and buggies and noisy cars. Arm in arm, Michael Green walked on the side closest to the street like the gentleman he was, and Celia strolled along closest to the boutiques and beautiful apartments, like the lady she was.

"There seem to be more and more motorized vehicles, haven't you noticed, Celia?" said Michael as they walked south. Indeed, they could count at least two Model Ts for every horse and carriage. From time to time, a tram would roll along and even a green double decker bus with its front spare tire covered by a

Mercedes Benz logo. At one point, a horse and carriage rolled by, and with it, a piece of horse dung flew up and caught Michael right on his coat. Celia laughed, hugged his arm, and looked up at him.

"That's why you're there, and I'm here," she said impishly, "to protect me from those dirty horses." Her laugh was like the tinkling of little bells. She radiated youth, beauty and happiness through her smile and wonderful personality. *Aren't I walking beside the most beautiful girl in New York?* Michael thought. Nodding right and left to other passers-by and neighbors that crossed his path, he grinned at his own good fortune.

"Michael, I know you're dying to tell me all about your amazing hometown," she said.
"I don't want to bore you."
"Don't be silly, Michael, I'm really interested in learning all I can while I'm in New York."

Michael thought about this, but after her dismal reaction on their trip downtown when he had tried to show Celia certain skyscrapers, he was not reassured. "Celia, I would love to tell you, but you did not seem overly impressed the last time."

"Those were office buildings, Michael. Who cares about workplaces? But here, with all these magnificent mansions, this is different. Anyway, I was impressed by that Gothic-style skyscraper you showed me. You know, the Woolworth, wasn't it?"

"Michael, who owns all these houses?"

"Some say it's the robber barons."

"Robber barons? That sounds intriguing, Michael. Are you a robber baron?"

"No, Celia, but that is a name given to the late 19th century businessmen who tended to create monopolies of all our major industries."

"Oh, you mean like my uncle George and his railroads?"

"Yes, I believe he was one of them, along with Jay Gould and Cornelius Vanderbilt in railroads, John D. Rockefeller in Standard Oil, J.P. Morgan and Andrew Carnegie in steel."

"Those are VIPs, aren't they? So, Michael, do they all have mansions here on Fifth Avenue?"

"Many do."

"Can we see them today?"

Michael nodded vaguely. Celia was very excited at this prospect. As for Michael, he was in his element. He hoped he could correctly remember the locations of the mansions but figured it would not really matter because Celia would not know if he was telling the truth.

"And the park, this magnificent Central Park? Has it always been here?" she asked, as her mind flitted from one subject to the next.

"Oh yes, it was created around 1857, and was based on Hyde Park in London, which is about 350 acres, I think. Ours is 840 acres, and therefore over twice the size of Hyde Park."

They continued to walk, and Michael had the feeling that he might be boring his companion with all these numbers, but he couldn't stop himself. At 67th Street, Michael said, "See this magnificent dwelling? This was Jay Gould's. Do you remember, I was talking about Jay Gould, the railroad tycoon?" But Celia was not listening because she was studying the dresses worn by a group of young women.

At 64th street, Michael said, "Celia, this is the Warburg mansion, you know the major international private bankers?" The word 'banker' seemed to jog something in her mind because she said,

"Like your father's?"

"Yes. Warburg is my father's major competitor."

"How exciting," said Celia. She wasn't excited, but she was curious, and for this, Michael was grateful.

On the corner of 62nd St., a little way down Fifth, Michael pointed to a five-story building behind twenty-foot-high gates. "See there? The Metropolitan Club, established by eighteen former members of the Union Club who objected to new money membership."

"Michael, are you new money?"

"No, the family has been wealthy for a long time."

"Does that mean your father is a member?"

"No, Celia, they would not want us."

"Really? I can't imagine why."

But Celia really didn't want to know so she quickly said, "What about the Vanderbilt mansion?"

"Oh Celia, that is a bit too far south to walk to. 57th Street, I think."

"Weren't you talking about the J.P. Morgan mansion?"

"It's too far to walk. I think that's at 36th street. Same with the Astor mansion, which is also farther south. You see, the older the money, the farther south the mansions."

"Is that really true, Michael?"

"Oh, I don't know. I just made it up," he said. Celia laughed and squeezed Michael's arm. Michael loved Celia's spontaneity because she made him feel good. And he could visualize his own self-importance through her eyes.

"I think it's time to turn around and walk back north," Michael said as they moved over to the west side of Fifth Avenue. They continued to walk, but Celia was now more interested in the women's fashions on display. Many women carried parasols to keep the strong sunlight from their faces, although their huge-brimmed hats were also fulfilling that function. They twirled their parasols and Celia imagined they were singing as they strolled along. "It seems like theater, Michael, or else they're walking in a parade. Is that the Russian pianist and composer Rachmaninoff?"

"I'm sorry, Celia, I can't help you there. Could be. There seem to be lots of famous people here today."

When they reached 91st Street, they stopped. "Celia, most of the nineteenth-century mansions that were built along Fifth Avenue were located between 60th and 70th streets. But this one was a trail blazer." Michael pointed to a Georgian style building on four floors that looked more like a city hall. "This is the Carnegie mansion, Andrew Carnegie. Carnegie owned practically all the steel industry in the U.S."

Celia smiled, "Lovely house. Would we live in such a place?" she asked. Michael was shocked. What on earth was Celia doing? *We?* He decided to ignore the comment. It was a beautiful Sunday afternoon, perfect for a Fifth Avenue parade. He heard there would be one soon, for the Suffragettes.

JAYNE LOUISE CRAMFORDE AND RICHARD BONTE

CHAPTER TWENTY – A FORK IN THE ROAD

Upper East Side, Davenport Mansion

It was a supposedly intimate Sunday affair—a delicious luncheon that had gone on for two hours—so that Celia and Don could be together. However, it was really a job interview for the task of being Celia's future husband and protector. George Davenport interviewed from his wheelchair behind this elongated Chippendale table, and Don Casterson was the interviewee. The maid had already removed the remnants of their Sunday rack of lamb, mint sauce, roasted potatoes, and French green peas. She was now serving coffee and brandy. In any other situation, Don would have wheeled Mr. Davenport to the living room so that they could sip their cognac together—between men, of course—and talk business. However, today, Celia was the 'business,' and very much involved, and thus, the interview continued in the dining room.

As Mr. Davenport thought about what he wanted to say, he contemplated the strapping young man in front of him. He remembered how he had once been a young and powerful physical specimen also, just like the opinionated and wealthy Don Casterson, comfortably installed at the head of the table. George's eyes wandered up to the long blue and silver swordfish on the wall directly above Don, and he remembered how he had wrestled it all by himself into his boat off the calm side of Barbados. That swordfish reminded him of how physically powerful he had once been, and ironically, how this was no longer the case. Even so, handicapped as he was, George Davenport had built an empire, the lavish details of which were reflected in his choice of furniture and art. He gazed with pride at the beautiful table setting the maid had laid, with its gold-rimmed plates and exquisite cutlery. His eyes wandered round the room as he remembered where he and Betty had bought the model sailing boats, bric-a-brac, Chinese lamps with their Tiffany light shades, and the Persian carpet. Would this young suitor prove as worthwhile a man as he?

"Don, what do you make of this interminable war in Europe?"

Don looked back at his lunch host and gathered his thoughts. "Well sir, I believe the U.S. should stay well clear of it. It's just another European civil war like the awful one we had some fifty years ago. To be

truthful, someone was assassinated, but that is no reason
to start a war."

There were only four of them seated at both ends
of this twenty-place dining table, but Don felt confident
in his answer and Mr. Davenport's trust in him. So
confident, in fact, that Don felt the urge to move his leg
so that it touched Celia's right leg under the table. Celia
moved hers away.

Betty Davenport, who was sitting on the opposite
side of the table with her husband, suddenly asked,

"Who is this Mata Hari woman that I have heard
about?"

Don answered, "She is a Belgium dancer who is
accused of spying for the Germans. If found guilty, they
will shoot her."

Betty looked shocked, "How awful! I wish you
had not told me."

Unseen, Don now placed his left hand on Celia's
right thigh. Celia used her right hand to remove Don's
and spoke, "Yes, Auntie, Don should know better. There
are certain things one should not say or do in polite
company." Celia turned to face Don and squinted her
eyes to show her disapproval. George nodded his head
admiringly at his plucky niece, and Betty had another
question,

"Who is this Rasputin fellow?" she asked. The
question was seemingly destined for Don, but George
answered,

"Some sort of advisor to the Czar, but I think he was shot by the Bolsheviks a few months ago."

"Oh George, more horrible information. You are as bad as Don."

Don grinned, and again placed his hand on Celia's thigh while Betty spoke,

"And who is this Lenin fellow? I read that he's returned to Russia after ten years in exile. And don't tell me someone shot him."

"No, he is still very much alive and will be causing incredible harm in Russia," George replied. "I believe he will be withdrawing Russia from the war."

"Surely that is a good thing?"

"Not really, Betty. Russia is in a terrible way. There are mass strikes and chaos after the royal family abdicated."

Don still had his hand on Celia's thigh. She did not remove it.

George looked at Don and said, "you really should consider moving to New York, especially while the economy is booming. We have recorded the highest profits in history, and if we enter the war, profits will be even higher."

Don was about to respond when he felt a sharp pain in his left hand as Celia stabbed him with her fork.

CHAPTER TWENTY-ONE – THE DRIVER

Central Park

    ... *"Yes, did I imagine it?"* Metz asked himself.

    "Did I touch the back of his neck? Did I really do that?" Celia asked herself. With her left hand still extended forward, Celia flew back in the seat as Metz accelerated into the park. Her left hand grabbed her right and quickly pushed down on her stomach as the Model T bounced along, the back seat springs thrusting up and under her. The trees and park benches whizzed by as she held her abdomen firm and imagined flying down a steep, snowy slope on her sleigh. Swish, bang, swish, swish, swish, ahhh. A cascade of falling snow and a wet spray of water.

    What would it be like? Would it be just as thrilling? Would it be painful? Or would it be passionate? It wouldn't be dull.

    These thoughts flashed through Celia's brain as the 'Central Park West' sign finally came into view. Then, the driver made a left turn, but all Celia could see now were two naked bodies tumbling over each other—over and over—in the grass as they rolled down a hill. Was she dreaming? She opened her eyes and squinted at the bright sunlight that had suddenly invaded the Model T. And out of the fire of the sunlight, out of the dancing flames, their two naked bodies shot up and just as soon faded away. Had she actually seen her wicked, naked body? Next to his? And would she be a virgin for very much longer? Would she be able to wait until she married? Yes, that was what she would do. She was sure of that. *I'll wait until my wedding night.*

"No!" She voiced her thoughts without meaning to.

"Sorry, Miss Celia, did you say something?"

"No."

"Have I done something wrong?" said the voice behind the strong forearms holding the wheel.

"No, Metz," said Celia, "no, you did nothing wrong. You could never do anything wrong. Oh no, no!"

"Are you alright, Miss Celia?" said Metz as he glanced in the rearview mirror and braked gradually outside her residence. Celia started shaking violently. Metz pulled to a final stop, and Celia lurched forward so that her left hand had to brace itself behind Metz' neck. She did all she could not to touch it again.

"If you are too cold, Miss Celia, I can get a blanket out of the trunk."

"Thank you, Metz, that would be a good idea."
She slowly withdrew her hand from the front seat but
continued to shake. She knew it was not the cool spring
air that had affected her. It was because she had
recognized the man in her daydream.

JAYNE LOUISE CRAMFORDE AND RICHARD BONTE

CHAPTER TWENTY-TWO – SAY NO MORE

Delmonico's on Fifth Avenue at 44th Street

The signature wedge-shaped building at the corner of Fifth and 44th beckoned the young couple into Delmonico's, the old-world restaurant that was the place to go in 1917 New York. Kings, statesmen, presidents, and other famous people dined on Delmonico's steaks, wedge salads, "Baked Alaska," Lobster Newberg, and other delicacies. Michael and Celia alighted from his Model T and made their way into the eleventh edition of the original Delmonico's that had started on Wall Street in 1827 with the Swiss-Italian immigrant brothers— Giovanni, and Pietro Delmonico.

"Look at these columns, Michael," said Celia.

Michael ran his hands along one of the massive columns by the front entrance and said, "Imported from the ruins of Pompeii, Celia, the ruins of Pompeii."

"From Italy?" Celia marveled.

"Just so, Madam," said the doorman, "Please come in and enjoy."

Inside, the fashionable eatery with its dark wood paneling and well-lit interior was packed with people. Waiters carrying large trays of food or drink scurried from kitchen to bar to table. There were frescoes everywhere and large potted ferns along the side walls. Celia and Michael followed, and hugged close to the maître d' who brought them to a corner table that overlooked the whole floor of the restaurant.

"Thank you, Luigi," said Michael, slipping a dollar bill into the maître d's tuxedo.

"What I wouldn't do for the Green family and their lovely friends," responded Luigi, smiling admiringly at Celia. He bowed to Michael and suavely pulled out Celia's chair for her. "Something to drink, my lady and gentleman?" Michael nodded, and Luigi immediately gesticulated to other attendant waiters to give Michael and Celia the royal treatment. Over the next hour and a half, they dined on seafood for Celia and steak for Michael, while three waiters attended to their every need.

"Oh Michael, this was such a good idea of yours to invite me to this most famous of famous restaurants. I've read about it. We don't have anything like this in Wichita." Celia suddenly clutched Michael's arm, "Michael, Michael," she whispered very loudly, "Isn't that our former president Teddy Roosevelt over there?" Celia nodded in the direction of a sixty-year-old gentleman in the other corner of the room.

"Yes, Celia, I believe it is. I'm so happy you like it here. Our family loves it, too. Established by Swiss Italians, you know, back in 1827."

"Oh Michael, I love everything about Europe, even though I've never been there. You have, haven't you?"

"Yes, Celia, many times. Before the war, our mother took us all, including our cook, to spend three months of the summer in London, and to my favorite seaside resort of Bournemouth, on the south coast of England."

"Oh please, tell me all about it. What is London like?"

"Well, Celia, do you know that London was started by the Romans in 43 B.C. as 'Londinium,' but now it is very much like Manhattan here?"

"Manhattan, New York City?"

"Yes. Most of it was built during the same time that New York was expanding and many of the buildings look the same. If you had a picture of a typical Fifth Avenue mansion and a similar size house in say, the Knightsbridge or Mayfair chic districts of London, you would not be able to tell which is which."

"Please Michael, I would so want to see London for myself. Would you take me there after the war has ended?"

Michael smiled a closed-lip smile and said nothing. On purpose. Then he looked at his watch and said, "It has been a wonderful meal. Come on, Celia, finish your Baked Alaska. I must return you to your Aunt Betty before the clock strikes eleven."

"Oh bother, do we have to go back so soon?"

"I'm afraid we must, Celia."

Celia snuggled up close to Michael on the way back. Michael felt very proud accompanying the most beautiful girl in Manhattan to her uncle's Fifth Avenue mansion that was only a few blocks north of his. They were upper class neighbors, and in a way, almost from the same school. He stopped in front of her residence, alighted, and walked around the car to open her door. He held her very close as they climbed the steps of her brownstone and approached the entrance.

"Michael, that was a lovely evening. Thank you so much." There was a pregnant pause. Celia waited for the response she hoped for.

"Miss Celia Dawes, may I kiss you goodnight?" Michael said.

"Mr. Michael Green, you have my permission."

Michael placed his right hand behind Celia's neck, and she did the same to his. They kissed. He smiled and held her at arm's length for a moment so he could admire her. Then, he carefully stepped down the steps and walked backwards to his car, always keeping Celia in his sight. She rang the doorbell. Michael waited in his car until the housekeeper had both let Celia into the house and closed the door along the hallway. Then, he drove off.

Inside, Celia continued towards the staircase and heard her aunt call out, "Celia dear, please join me for a moment."

"Of course, Aunt Betty."

Betty kissed Celia and held her at arm's length, a bit like Michael had done earlier. "Did you have a good time, darling?"

"Yes, I did, Auntie, Michael is so nice."

"Well, that's wonderful, darling. Listen, my dear. Listen to your old Auntie. Now, I don't want to meddle in your life, you know that? Meddling is the last thing I would want to do. However, I must say that you shouldn't get too involved with Mr. Green."

Celia blushed deeply as she realized Aunt Betty must have seen her kiss Michael. "But Auntie, surely Michael is a respectable young man. What could possibly go wrong?"

"My dear," began Betty. She seemed to be very ill at ease, "Celia, I must trust you to ensure nothing serious comes of this?"

"I'm sorry? Serious?"

"Yes, my dear. Now, Don Casterson is an obvious choice for a partner. He went to Yale. He's a good Yale man."

"But Michael is a Yale man, too."

"Yes, Celia, but, well, let's say it's different."

"Different, different, Auntie? Different in what way. They are both incredibly wealthy, aren't they? At least their families are very wealthy, isn't that the case?"

"Yes, my dear, but...well...if you were to marry Michael, you...you wouldn't be welcome at some of the best country clubs, for example. Oh, this is so difficult for me to say."

"Country clubs?"

"Well, yes, Celia, and many other social gatherings, too."

"But what do you mean, Auntie? What are you trying to say?" Celia shouted. "Why? Why?"

"Oh Celia, it's not your fault, but you are so naïve. You don't have these people around you there in Wichita, I guess."

"*These* people?"

"Oh, Celia, the Greens are delightful people, really delightful, but we rarely mix socially."

"What do you mean, Auntie? What about the party we attended?"

"Well, yes, they have amazing parties, but marriage would be so difficult, and such a problem."

"Again, why, Auntie?"

"Oh Celia, can't you see, can't you understand who these people are? They are, well, they're not Protestants, I can say that. There, I've said it."

"Are they Catholics?"

"Oh no, Celia, no."

"Then what are they?" Celia yelled.

"They're far worse, my dear."

"Oh."

JAYNE LOUISE CRAMFORDE AND RICHARD BONTE

CHAPTER TWENTY-THREE – GRASS IS GREENER

Midtown Manhattan

Don and Celia sailed down Fifth Avenue through the sixties and seventies, but when they approached the thirties, traffic slowed to a crawl. Don stretched his neck out the side to look beyond the horse and buggy stuck behind a line of cars in front of him.

"Ten years ago, we were one of the few families with an automobile. Now look at us. The proles have come into the picture, and they've invaded Fifth Avenue," he said.

"Are we in a rush, Don?" said Celia.

Don flashed a big smile as he sped round the horse and buggy and three cars in front, "See that? Now, that's what I call 'driving,' if I don't say so myself. You asked me if we were in a rush?" Don pulled up and stopped with a jerk on the southeast corner of Fifth and 37th St.

"Don, why are we stopping here?"

"It's your birthday. Have you forgotten?"

"It's not my birthday," said Celia.

"It's your birthday every day, as far as I'm concerned." Don had walked round the front of the car and opened the passenger door. "Here we are at Tiffany's," he said proudly, extending both arms up at a seven-story, wedge-shaped building. "Look at those magnificent Corinthian columns, and the iron and marble exterior. It's got that South London or Oxford Street style. Not to speak of what's inside, for you, Miss Celia Dawes."

"But Don, I told you, it's not my birthday. And besides, anything here would be far too expensive for a gift. Please, Don. You're embarrassing me."

"But I insist, Miss Celia. And when I want something for you, you will have it, believe me."

"No, Don. Please. If you really want to give me something, how about some small gift like say, from B. Altman? Their department store is close by, isn't it? Or a small store on Ladies Mile at 14th or 16th street? That is where I usually shop with my aunt."

"Would you be comfortable if we went to Lord & Taylor?"

"Yes, Don. Good choice."

They stepped back into the Model T and drove south. Then, they turned right at 20th Street and continued to the Broadway intersection and stopped at number 901. Don jumped out and opened the door for Celia again. He gestured grandly at the eleven-story, Italian Renaissance Revival style commercial building, and they walked in. Then, he spread his arms out again.

"Lord & Taylor. Anything you want in the store is yours, Celia."

"Anything?"

"Yes, anything because you are everything, Celia. You are worth everything."

"That is so sweet of you, Don. That is so nice." She looked around and the ladies glove department caught her eye. "Let's see. Anything. How about a pair of gloves? Yes, that's it, a pair of gloves."

"What? No jewelry?"

"No Don, thank you, just gloves."

"Alright then, Celia, as long as your gloves are the most expensive pair in the store."

Celia was radiant because she was certain she had found Mr. Right. He was everything a girl could want. He was smart, confident, empathetic, and a real go-getter. He was also very handsome.

Celia began to finger the different selections of fine kid gloves when she happened to look up and see a young couple walking along the sidewalk. A dark cloud came over her face. *That can't be Metz, can it? And who's the young woman walking with him?*

JAYNE LOUISE CRAMFORDE AND RICHARD BONTE

CHAPTER TWENTY-FOUR – CARLA SIGNORI

Plaza Hotel, Manhattan

The Model T taxicab bounced along north on Fifth Avenue and onto Central Park South where the Renaissance-style chateau, the Plaza Hotel reigned supreme. Andrew Smith, Don Casterson's bachelor friend visiting from Chicago, hopped out, paid the driver, and made his way up to suite 301 on the third floor. Without knocking, he thrust open the door to find Don sprawled out in an armchair with his feet propped up on an ottoman. Next to Don was a bottle of Chivas and two scotch glasses on the table.

"Don!" he exclaimed.

"Andy, Andrew," said Don as he jumped up and gave his best friend from Yale a handshake and tap on the arm. "Not too tired, I hope?" said Don. "We've got work to do. Here, have a drink."

"How long you got this room for?" said Andrew.

"Just for tonight. That's all the time we need, my friend, just like the old days after football."

"So, what do you have planned for tonight?" said Andrew, sipping the stiff drink Don had tendered.

"Well, Andrew, we could go to the theater. There's a play on with that actor Boris Karloff, or we could catch a vaudeville with the Marx Brothers, or even comedian Jack Benny."

"I'm talking girls, Don, got any of those?"

"That's for afterwards, Big Fellow," said Don, "let's set the stage first."

"Is Fanny Brice appearing anywhere in New York?" asked Andrew.

"No, but Al Johnson's on Broadway."

"I don't think so. Well, Don, that leaves the slumming option. How 'bout the flee pits?"

"Motion pictures? I guess. I could go for a Mary Pickford or Douglas Fairbanks -"

"They always play together, Don."

"Right, and they always enact some ridiculous feat on screen. If not, how about a Mae West?"

"Wait a minute, Don, I have it. You're right, it has to be a film tonight. Look, let's see if there's a Carla Signori film playing. Get us in the mood for afterwards. God, she is so beautiful and sexy. What wouldn't I give to spend a night with her?"

Don changed countenance. He hesitated, tried to collect his thoughts. Should he pretend or brag? Would Andrew believe him if he told him the truth? Don decided to keep quiet, at least for now, but the memory came flooding back. He felt light-headed and needed a chair to sit on. He plopped back on the armchair and inclined backwards.

"Sure, Andrew, the Carla Signori movie sounds like a good choice. Afterwards, we'll have some champagne."

"Champagne?" said Andrew. "What are we celebrating?"

"Well, nothing really, Andy, I was just thinking about an old girlfriend."

"Girlfriend, Don? Which one? Haven't I met them all?"

"Yes, but, umm, not actually the one I'm thinking about."

"You've got me intrigued there. Was she beautiful? Blonde, brunette, or a redhead? No answer? Don? We're not talking some black whore, are we?"

Don's face suddenly flushed red. "Of course not, Andy. Don't be ridiculous."

Unnoticed by the boisterous Andrew, Don was quiet as they entered the Broadway movie theater on the Upper West Side. Ten minutes into the film, Don realized he was not following the story on the text cards. Instead, he was staring at Carla Signori. Her presence was magnetic and dwarfed that of her fellow actors who appeared to be mere shadows in comparison, but there was something else going on. Don's own private film of her had taken over in his mind. *He saw a stunning dark-skinned young woman in her mid-teens washing his feet. She kissed them, caressed them. She wore a thin, white cotton dress that seemed to become progressively wetter as soapy water from her pail splashed up and left big wet marks over her nipples that stood erect and black under the fabric. He glanced down and noticed a dark shadow of pubic hair between her thighs. She undid the top buttons of his pants.*

"Do you know what the gossip columnists say about Carla Signori?" said Andrew. Don jumped and shook in his seat. Andrew answered his own question. "That she is not really Italian, but black, and she used to be a whore here in New York."

Don said nothing, but shook silently in the dark, as tears streamed down his face.

CHAPTER TWENTY-FIVE – METZ-O

East Eksteen, Long Island

Driving slowly down a very long dirt road winding out to the shore, they saw a nineteenth-century mansion of cut limestone, resplendent in the morning sun. Sitting almost on the beach itself, the mini château lay only two hundred feet from the Long Island Sound and cast an immense shadow over the water separating East Eksteen from West Eksteen. It was an excellent copy of a magnificent Napoleon III country home, largely resembling the Château de Monte Cristo, near Paris. It belonged to one Stanislas Parker, who was a very big deal in the New York City banking community.

Stanislas Parker was George Davenport's good friend and business partner. Mr. Parker's wife, Georgia, was also very well connected and had organized a season-opening party for their daughter, an only child. Cassandra Parker was the same age as Celia and of similar disposition. That is, both girls loved parties, especially luxurious parties in their parents' second houses. And Celia had insisted her uncle allow Metz to drive her there in his recently acquired Rolls Royce Phantom to create a stir. However, at 11 am in the morning, the only stir was from the gardeners going about their business outside on the vast grounds— mowing, cutting, and cleaning up from the night before. It was now late spring on Long Island and New Yorkers were spending more and more time in their summer homes.

Metz entered the circular driveway and pulled up to the front entrance. The sun from the east glittered off the windows set into the heavy French doors. His eyes shone a deep green in the reflection, as did Celia's eyes a light blue. Metz jumped up to help Celia dismount, who willingly leaned on him more than was necessary,

"Oh, Metz, you do know I had to beg my uncle to let you drive me here, don't you? Uncle Georgie's idea of a good time now is staying inside in New York and doing crossword puzzles. And I don't want Auntie Betty hanging over me like a dark cloud all the time. Oh, look, it is so picturesque here. The ocean beckons us, Metz."

"Might be a little bit cold this time of year, Miss Celia."

"Maybe so, but the sea air is divine." Celia turned around and saw someone at the entrance. "Cassie?" An attractive young woman of eighteen, Cassandra DeVille, along with two middle-aged servants, approached.

"Oh Cassie, it's beautiful here. You are so lucky?"

"I know, Celia, welcome to East Eksteen," said Cassandra. "We have so many fun things to do today. We'll play croquet, and there is a tennis court on the side—you can't see it from here but take my word for it—and there's my big birthday party tonight."

"I know. It will be wonderful, Cassie. And you're just eighteen. I guess I'm the older woman here." Celia looked imperiously at Metz. "This is my driver, Metz. Can you show him where to go?"

"Certainly, Celia," said Cassandra. "Hello, Mr. Metz. This is Mr. Bukowski and his wife, Agnieszka. Please show Mr. Metz around. You both must be famished after your long trip."

"See you later, Metz," Celia called out as Metz left with the servants. "Remember, we must leave at eleven pm to return to New York."

Metz liked this arrangement. Parker's Polish servants were kind, simple folk who fed him well, and then showed him the mansion, the grounds, the stables, and the collection of antique cars Mr. Parker had collected. Throughout this time, Metz engaged in light banter with everyone, but he was secretly trying to better understand the game of life. The game of life as played by the rich. How was it some people had all the goodies and others didn't? Parker owned several cars plus a silver Rolls Royce from 1907, whereas Davenport owned a 1917 Rolls Phantom. How was it that these cars were just discardable toys to these VIPs whereas for him, the acquisition of such a 'toy' represented a lifetime dream? Metz learned that buying quality—like a Rolls Royce, for example—was what rich people did. They did not buy junk. Metz carefully observed the other habits and leisure activities of the ultra-rich. And he came to the unescapable conclusion that it was really quite simple. Metz needed to make a lot of money if he ever were to enjoy the goodies of life. In his opinion, money wasn't everything; it was the only thing, and if he couldn't find a way of getting rich quickly, he would always remain a servant of the rich.

With so much to see and so much to do, the day went by very quickly for both Metz and Celia. At eleven p.m., Metz waited in the Rolls for a slightly tipsy Celia, who did all she could to walk a straight line. Supported on both sides by Agnieszka and Piotr Bukowski, she waved a sloppy goodbye to Cassandra Parker, and walked unsteadily to the car. Metz jumped out immediately to help guide Celia into the Rolls. Celia clung to Metz as he placed her in the back seat.

Metz was certain that Celia would be fast asleep by the time he resumed driving. He looked in the mirror to see her head resting peacefully on the head rest. However, before they were to regain the main road back to Manhattan, Celia ordered Metz to pull off to the side, stop the car, and attend to her. She was having "problems" with something, and she needed his help. She had wedged her foot under the front seat and her shoe had gotten stuck. But as Metz tried to remove her shoe, Celia calmly slipped her foot out and ran it slowly up his thigh. Like a veteran Geisha girl, she left her foot there, close to the vital spot while she massaged his thigh, ever so slowly with her toes. Then, she extended her beautiful arms out and took Metz' rough hands in hers, kneading his forearms while continuing to massage his thigh with her foot. There was not a car on the road, and the trees formed a perfect cover for what was to happen next.

"Take me, darling Metz," she whispered, "take me in your big broad forearms and make me a woman. Only you can do it. I want you now, Metz."

Metz could not resist her, and for the next hour, he had to cover her mouth as she screamed the pleasures of the damned.

JAYNE LOUISE CRAMFORDE AND RICHARD BONTE

CHAPTER TWENTY-SIX – UNREQUITED

Davenport Mansion – Fifth Avenue

Late the next afternoon, the sky was cheerless. Light clouds had gathered, but it did not look like it was going to rain. Celia had appeared on the porch and looked imperiously out onto the street where Metz, sporting a black Kijima oversized beret, stood at attention next to the Model T, and gazed up at her.

Upon her return from the party the night before, she had taken a long bath and gone to sleep. She had gotten up late, eaten breakfast and exchanged pleasantries with her aunt and uncle, and then returned to her room 'to experience her new self.' She wrote in her diary, brushed her hair repeatedly, and went about her everyday business. As she had been physically consumed the night before, she moved about as much as possible to maintain her equilibrium, or so she thought. She felt a tingling in her abdomen that extended throughout her body, and up into her fingertips. She sat upright and felt it in her smile as she looked at herself in the mirror, brushing and re-brushing her hair that glowed and shone more than normal. Her expression had changed—for that, she could be sure—and when she looked deep into her eyes, she thought she could see waves of white froth playing lightly over a deep blue sea. She absolutely glowed with heat and pleasure. She stood up and stared at her image in the full-length mirror. She knew she was stunning, even if she never said so out loud. And when she delved more carefully into her new image, she realized that yesterday she had left New York as 'Mademoiselle,' but last night, she had returned as 'Madame.'

She gathered her hat and a small matching purse, tugged at her skirt to examine her shoes, and strode out into the living room.

"You look beautiful," said Betty.

"Thank you, Auntie, for the wonderful compliment. Has Metz brought out the car?"

"Yes, he's waiting outside for you. Have fun," said George as he continued to work on a crossword puzzle. She then bade goodbye to her aunt and uncle with a careless "See you later," and walked outside.

Metz ascended the stairs halfway to the porch where he met Celia coming down.

"How are you, Metz?" Celia said, but she held on to the railing rather than take his hand.

"As well as could be expected, Miss Celia."

He followed her and helped her into the back seat. When he resumed his spot behind the wheel, she said, "Would you take me to the Casterson residence, Metz? You know where it is, don't you?"

"Yes, Miss Celia, I do," he responded.

JAYNE LOUISE CRAMFORDE AND RICHARD BONTE

CHAPTER TWENTY-SEVEN – OVERSIZED BERET

Don Casterson watched from his living room as a Model T pulled up outside. The driver, a well-built young man wearing a black Kijima oversized beret, jumped out and ran over to the passenger side to help Celia alight. She nodded curtly to the driver, who resumed his spot behind the wheel and drove off slowly. Don grabbed his brown felt Homburg and rushed down to see her. He met Celia as she was about to ring the front bell. Don opened the door quickly and stood in front of it.

"Why didn't you ring me? I would have picked you up?" said Don.

"I was just about to ring you," said Celia. "Aren't you going to invite me in?"

"Well, yes, but weren't we supposed to meet your friend, Cassandra Parker, and her boyfriend, at the restaurant? That's what you told me last time we talked."

"It's not really her boyfriend," said Celia. "Just some fellow she met."

"Well, it's almost one. We'll be late," said Don. He grabbed her by the hand and rushed her downstairs. "Come on, let's take the roadster."

Don sped around corners and drove his 1917 yellow roadster much too fast for Celia's liking. But they were late, and it was her fault and so, she did not complain.

"What's this new interest in Cassandra Parker?" said Don over the street noise.

"She threw a wonderful party in East Eksteen this past weekend. So please, don't let her boyfriend pay for food at the restaurant. That's the least I can do for her in exchange."

"Sure, no problem, Celia. So, this Cassandra Parker has a place in East Eksteen? That's expensive. How old is she?" said Don.

"Well, no, it's not her. It's her dad who threw the party. I think East Eksteen's his second or third home, I'm not sure. He lives in Manhattan."

"How did you get there? Did your driver take you? That guy that drove you here?"

"Yes, Don, what do you think of him?"

"Your driver?"

"His name is Metz. What do you think of him?" said Celia again.

"Who cares, Celia? He's just your driver. Getting back to 'Cassandra,' is it? Isn't that Stanislas Parker's daughter, you know, Stanislas Parker of Chemical Bank?" Don said, as they careened to a stop.

"Cassie? Yes, and her dad would be a very good business contact for you. So be nice to her. She's cute, too. I don't think it will be hard." The traffic controller signaled for Don to go, and Don slammed on the accelerator pedal.

"Would you mind not driving so fast?" Celia said.

"What's it to you?" said Don. "You want to get there, don't you?"

"Yes, Don, but in one piece."

"Oh, in one piece?" Don accelerated in response. "In one piece?"

"Please, Don!" Celia screamed.

"Come on, Celia, lighten up." Don slowed down to a crawl. "Is that how your driver—what's his name— 'Metz' drives? Like an old man?"

"Don't tell me you're jealous of Metz now, are you?" said Celia.

"Jealous of your servant driver 'Metz' that wears a gorilla beret? Are you kidding me?"

"Gorillas are good for certain things," said Celia. "What?"

"Don, I said that Metz is a very careful driver."

"There," said Don, bowling to a stop in front of the restaurant. "That took all of ten minutes. You're right on time."

But Celia didn't listen to a word he said. She waved to Cassandra Parker and a fellow Celia remembered from the party, and who had just pulled up in another Dodge, a green Model 30 roadster.

CHAPTER TWENTY-EIGHT – FAST TRACK

Hester Street, Manhattan

"You boys are looking tired; can I tell you that?" said Mrs. Lubelski. Lefty Goldstein and Metz had never hit it off at the 'Polack House,' as they called it. Metz was basically an optimist with a sense of humility and deprecation. Lefty was a small kid who slept all morning, worked security in the Garment District in the afternoon and at a meat packing plant on graveyard shift. He was angular and mean, and always saw the crummy side of things. They often met in the kitchen when Lefty was going to work, and James was coming back from work.

"You know I always have your good at heart, but I think they're working you boys too hard," said Mrs. Lubelski.

"Don't worry about us, Mrs. Lubelski, we're still young," said Lefty.

"You tellin' me I'm old?" said Mrs. Lubelski.

"We love ya, Mrs. Lubelski, you know that," said Metz.

"Whatever. Gotta run," said Lefty. Lefty flew out the door and down the stairs.

"What a depressing boy he is," said Mrs. Lubelski.

"Lefty's doin' graveyard, Mrs. Lubelski, that's probably why. That kind of work might get you down. Anyway, I was just about to take a nap," said Metz, with one hand on the door handle of his room.

"You do that, my boy. It will do ya the world of good. Put some hair on your chest. You wanna read today's "New York Times?" We've all been through it."

"Thank you. It looks it," said Metz, as he took the dirty newspaper in his greasy hands. There were bits of egg on it, a couple of coffee stains, the paper was crumpled, but the print was readable enough. "See you later, Mrs. Lubelski."

Metz closed his door, but it seemed as if he hadn't closed it with all the noise blasting in from the street and Mrs. Lubelski herself. He loved "Mrs. L," but for some reason, she always had to sing loudly in Polish when he took his daily nap. Metz figured she kept herself company while she cleaned the dishes. He couldn't understand this way of hers because she told him he looked tired, and that he should get more sleep, and then she started singing. In addition, he could hear automobile horns honk, horses neigh, and scores of loud immigrants close their stands for the day to go home. He would overhear sixty languages a day he couldn't understand, nor did he want to.

Metz looked around at his filthy room. At the dirty green walls that had turned grey, the dusty wood floor caked with grease from the kitchen next door, and his moth-eaten blanket that was of little use. *It stinks here; I can do better than this,* he thought, *but how?*

At this point, Mrs. Lubelski stopped singing and shouted at one of the Polish lodgers. An argument ensued. *What a horrible language Polish is,* Metz said to himself. He lay back on his bed and picked up the newspaper Mrs. Lubelski had given him.

"Moody Schwartzman donates $10,000 to a Jewish children's hospital," went the headline. The article only cited good things about Moody Schwartzman. *Isn't this the same guy who rigs ball games?* Metz thought. *What's better? Paying someone to lose a ballgame or helping a kid? Gotta get the money somehow, I s'pose.*

Metz threw the article aside and thought about Celia. He couldn't believe how she'd just tossed her virginity aside to "mate" with him. Because that's what he called it. *It was fantastic, but it certainly wasn't making love.* She hadn't even mentioned the incident in the Rolls when he saw her the next day. As if it had never happened. And then he had to drive her to see

137

these different guys like Michael Green or Don Casterson. *Is she poking them, too? I don't think so.* Metz had to think that over. He knew he had devirginized her. He'd had to remove blood from all over the back seat before he took the old man out early the next morning. *The grumpy old man hadn't even mentioned his niece's party. That was probably a good thing.* Metz smiled to himself because he reasoned that Celia was probably not having sex with the other two, and that he, Metz, had a leg up on them, literally and figuratively. However, Green and Casterson both had one huge advantage over him. Money. If Metz were to have any chance with Celia, he would need to get rich quickly. As good as the sex was in the back of the Rolls, she would get used to it, and he would be regulated to a 'mating bull' role. *That's not so bad,* he reasoned. However, he was more than a driver, mechanic and 'mating bull.' Metz was a good person, and he had a lot going for him. But he was in the rat race, going in circles. He needed a way out to the fast track. Maybe he should meet Moody Schwartzman. *Can the Jew give me some pointers about how to get rich quick?* However, Metz also knew that Moody Schwartzman was a fraud and a bad man. And Metz also knew himself, and that he was not like that. *Yes,* he said to himself, *Moody's obviously a crook.*

Is it true that behind every fortune there's a crime?

CHAPTER TWENTY-NINE – METZ, JAMES METZ

Washington Square, Lower Manhattan

Just south of Fifth Avenue, Metz walked along Waverly Place to enter Washington Square. The trees provided a green velvet blanket over the Manhattan landmark on this particularly warm spring day. Metz meandered in cool comfort along its curving paths next to the statues of Italian patriot, Giuseppe Garibaldi, or the savior of the American steel industry, engineer Alexander Lyman Holley. There were children running about and men playing chess at two separate tables. Metz looked up to see the Washington Square Arch standing tall at the north end of the square. It was made of tuckahoe marble and modeled after the French Arc de Triomphe in Paris. These were soldiers' arches, war memorials. Metz thought about men of his age fighting over in France and wondered when the hostilities would ever end. When Metz came to the horizontal

139

overhanging branch of Hangman's Elm, he decided he'd sit down for a while on a long park bench beside the tree and have a think.

But Metz didn't notice that there was a man in his late forties sitting on the other end of the bench and reading a small book of some kind. The man was dressed rather oddly, in a faded red shirt that had almost gone pink, a blue cloth tie, a long overcoat, black bowler hat, and black shoes. His complexion was pasty, and his hair overlong.

Metz finally noticed the man and regretted sitting down because it looked like this man might engage him in conversation. This was the last thing Metz wanted. However, Metz felt it would be rude to stand up and walk away suddenly, so he looked out into the distance and gathered his thoughts.

Meanwhile, the man had looked at Metz when he sat down. Metz realized he would never have any privacy and was about to walk away, when the other man said, "Excuse me, young man, would you be so kind as to read this for me? I don't seem to have brought my glasses with me." Metz gathered the man was English from his accent. The English gentleman then walked over to Metz' side, sat down, and presented Metz a play script. Metz looked from the man to the script and back to the man again.

"I guess? What did you want me to read?" said Metz.

"This page. This character," said the man. Metz looked at the man with hesitation, but then he read the play text, word by word, with no intonation, and with no understanding. "Thank you," said the man. "I just wanted to hear it read. Do you know that a good-looking man like you could be a movie star? Have you ever considered that possibility?"

"No, sir," said Metz.

"Allow me to introduce myself. My name is Horace Harmsworth, and I've been brought over from England to be an acting coach in the theater. I think you have the look to be a theater or movie star, and I could help you with your acting skills if you'd like?" said Mr. Harmsworth.

"Funny, no one's ever told me that," said Metz.

"Well, yes, I really think so."

"Sir, Mr. Harmsworth, I'm sorry, I've never thought of being an actor and frankly, I can't afford anything," said Metz.

"Let's put it this way," replied Harmsworth, "Let's say my fee would be deferred indefinitely, and is contingent on your becoming a star."

"Star?" said Metz. "I guess? That is very generous of you, but I just don't see myself as an actor. Thank you for the compliment anyway, Mr. Harmsworth." Metz stood up, and was about to walk away when he turned around and said, "Do you think I could act the part of a very wealthy and successful businessman?"

"I don't see why not. I could easily help you do that," said Harmsworth, giving Metz a card. Metz looked it over for a bit and then looked up,

"Well, thank you, Mr. Harmsworth. My name's Metz, Jimmy Metz, but I don't have a card."

"That's alright, Mr. Metz. Call me soon. And by the way, the first lesson is, "My name is Metz, James Metz."

"Yes, thank you, sir. I'll remember that. 'Metz, James Metz.'"

CHAPTER THIRTY – MR. RIGHT

Righton's Polo Club, Long Island, New York

Holding a pink parasol above an enormous wide-brimmed hat with three bird feathers, Celia paced up the field sideline following the polo teams dressed in red and blue. A man on the red team galloping up the right wing glanced to his left and spotted Don Casterson thundering up the middle towards the goal. The winger sent a nice little pass just to the right of Don's horse. Don cocked his mallet and slammed the wooden ball home. The scorekeeper put up a slate reading '5' for the reds and '4' for the blues.

"Great shot," Celia screamed, "Great shot."

"Nice goal," Geri Southern shouted, "Nice goal, Don."

Soon after, horse and riders retired to the back of the field. An announcement was made:

"Ladies and Gentlemen, it is half time. Please be so kind as to walk across the field before you return to the Clubhouse. Yes, you heard that correctly. Walk on the field and replace as many divots as you can." There was a loud coughing noise through the loudspeaker and the same man's voice could be heard whispering, "What's that? Tell them to bring their drinks?" The man cleared his throat, and his voice resumed its normal tenor as he said, "And yes, by all means take your drinks with you, but please, remember to replace as many divots as you can."

Celia and Geri began their walk along the field. Celia's hat, like her parasol, was tinged with pink. She wore a long, Morphew collection white lace dress with medium-heeled pumps. Geri didn't have a parasol, but she sported a wide-brimmed hat with blue feathers, along with a light blue cotton day dress.

"Bet I can jump on more of these misplaced pieces of turf than you can," said Celia, jumping on a particularly large divot.

"Bet you can't," said Geri, rising to the challenge.

The young ladies ran and jumped on stray bits of turf dug up by the horses. They hooted and laughed, and generally made a spectacle of themselves. The other staider patrons gave the girls dirty looks as they discreetly smoothed down the divots on the field. Geri glanced up to see another girl the same age looking down on her.

"That's enough, Celia," said Geri, shooting another glance at the judgmental girl. Celia turned to see who Geri was looking at and took Geri's arm.

"You're right," she whispered, "We need to behave. I am eighteen years old now and should be thinking about whom I'm going to marry."

"Don't rush into anything, Celia." Celia laughed.

"So, my sixteen-year-old friend is now the sage?"

"Yes, I think so," said Geri.

"Alright, then," said Celia, "Maybe you can help me choose." Celia looked across the field and spotted Don chatting with the winger who had sent him the winning pass. She waved to Don, who waved back.

"Well, actually I know already," said Celia. She waved to Don again. "It's him, Don over there. I know Don Casterson is the best choice. He's of good stock, from a proud Chicago family. He's obviously wealthy, although who cares? Wealth doesn't matter."

"What?" said Geri, as they approached the Clubhouse. "What is this nonsense, 'wealth doesn't matter?' How 'bout if you're poor?"

"Well naturally, Geri, everyone needs a minimum to live on."

"What is a minimum, Celia?"

"Oh, I don't know. A million dollars?"

"What about the other men? You said you needed to 'choose.' How 'bout that one you've secretly been seeing?" Celia's face turned so red, her pink hat and dress looked white in comparison. *She knows my secret.* Without a beat, Celia responded,

"I assume you're referring to Michael Green?"

"Why yes, of course, is there another one you haven't told me about?"

"Oh no, never, of course not, Geri. You're my best friend. You're the first person I would tell if that were the case."

"So, what about this Mr. Green?" said Geri, "Wouldn't he be a good candidate? He's handsome, and he also comes from a very wealthy family. How old is he?"

"Nineteen, I think," said Celia.

"Seems a bit young," said Geri, "You're better off with the more mature Casterson."

"I think so," said Celia. "And mother would definitely approve of him. He's the 'right sort' of man if you know what I mean?"

"Oh yes, of course, Celia. Apparently, Michael's mother is rumored to be of that persuasion? Such a shame, really. Especially since they are all so cultured."

"Yes," Celia sighed with relief. *Geri doesn't know.*

CHAPTER THIRTY-ONE – REQUITED LOVE

Sitting in the back seat of the Model T, Celia barely noticed the ferry ride taking her from New York City across the Hudson to New Jersey. She was deep in thought.

Ever since the night of the party in the car, Celia had been thinking of Metz. In the days following this defining moment, Metz drove her dutifully about from place to place, and from Michael to Don, or Don to Michael, and they exchanged nothing but polite 'niceties' with each other. *The silence is deafening* went the cliché, and it was painful, and it was real. It pained her to pretend not to like him. She was sad to not speak to him, or not acknowledge him, as he went about his duties at the Davenport household. From time to time, she would wander around the house and run into Metz doing some lowly chore or working on one of the three Davenport automobiles. The estranged lovers would catch each other's eye, and Celia would invariably look away. Why was she doing this to herself? And to him? She had witnessed the sadness in his eyes, the confusion in his face as he invariably thought, *"What have I done wrong?"* But of course, he had done nothing wrong. On the contrary, he had done everything right. And when she returned home from a date with Michael or Don, or when she went to a play or the movies with her aunt, there was always the stoic Metz. She gazed with wonder at this man in front of her. She marveled at his strong forearms attached to the steering wheel, his limpid blue gaze taking in everything around him.

This was the moment. Would Celia proceed? The thoughts rushed through her mind. *Don't be such a fool. Go home. Just say, "I can't."* Then, as she looked at Metz, all such doubts were swept away.

"Is it far yet, Metz?" she said, from her imperious perch in the back seat.

"Not so much, Miss Celia, we're almost there," he answered.

The Bridgewater Inn of Pleasure Bay, Long Branch, New Jersey was close enough to the Jersey shore, but far enough from Manhattan, to be the perfect spot for Celia.

"You're going to have to stop calling me 'Miss Celia' soon," said Celia.

"And you're going to have to stop calling me 'Metz,'" said Metz.

"Isn't it exciting?" Celia cried, louder than she had intended.

"Yes, Miss Celia, I'm looking forward to it."

"I'm dying for it, Metz. You must know that. By the way, you haven't been here before, have you?"

"Oh no," Metz lied, as he remembered the last time he'd driven out to the shore. While he and a date were going up to their room, Metz had made friends with this frail-looking bellhop, Guido. The friendship had had a funny beginning. Metz noticed that Guido was shaking and very upset. Apparently, a Jersey gang member had just robbed the bellhop of a five-dollar tip he'd received from some millionaire. "Where is he?" Metz demanded. The bellhop quickly took them back down to the lobby where they spotted the gang member in a parking lot. Metz ran after the gang member, recovered the five dollars, broke the fellow's nose, and told him he'd kill him if he ever bothered Guido again. Guido had never forgotten this kind gesture.

"I have a friend who works here," Metz finally answered Celia's lingering question. "His name is Guido, and he'll do anything for me, I mean, for us."

"You know I love you, don't you, Metz?"

"Thank you, Miss Celia, you have a funny way of showing it sometimes."

They alighted in front of the majestic Bridgewater Inn, a country inn with gables, Corinthian columns, and a wide front porch. An American flag waved in the breeze as Celia, dressed in a simple white cotton dress and wide-brimmed hat, and Metz, in an old but clean topcoat and tails, walked up the front steps to the reception area. Guido was there and overjoyed to see his protector. He led the couple to a side room with nothing but a long table, covered in a clean white cloth. On one side of the table was a Bible and two gold bands on a small, silver tray. On the other side was a bottle of red wine and three glasses.

A clergyman dressed in black beckoned to them. Guido assumed a somber air and stood at one side of the table. The clergyman spoke,

"God, we are gathered here to enter James Metz and Celia Dawes into Holy Matrimony," he said to the couple. "Celia and James, please approach the table. Now, each of you place your right hand on the Bible. Celia placed her right hand first, and James covered it with his. The clergyman continued in a solemn tone, "Do each of you solemnly swear to love each other, look out for each other, in sickness and in health, till death do you part?"

"We do," came the joint response.

Then, they separated and turned towards each other. The clergyman then addressed Metz and intoned,

"James Holstein Metz, do you take Celia Marie Dawes to be your lawful wedded wife?"

"I do," said Metz.

"Celia Marie Dawes, do you take James Holstein Metz to be your lawful wedded husband?"

"I do," said Celia.

"Then, by the grace of God Almighty, I pronounce you man and wife. You may kiss the bride, Mr. Metz." The two lovers kissed hungrily. "Congratulations to the two of you," said the clergyman.

"Room 201, Guido?" said Celia.

"Right, but first have a glass of wine on me."

They moved to the other side of the table. Guido uncorked the wine, poured three glasses, and cheered, "Congratulations to Mr. and Mrs. James Metz!"

All three drank to each other's happiness. James and Celia downed their drinks in one shot, while Guido sipped his.

"Thank you so much, Guido!" Celia let out.

James grabbed Celia by the hand, and they ran up the wooden staircase as fast as they could to Room 201. They tore off their clothes and jumped into bed. Neither had time to remove their shoes.

Celia had waited weeks for this, "Oh James, James Holstein Metz, I do love you so, so much. There will never be another."

"And I love you, my darling Celia Marie Metz."

"You see, we're on an equal level now— Oh my God! Oh, Great God!" Celia screamed, as James entered her.

"I love you, sweet Celia, I always have."

And with that, they made mad, passionate love, lunging and sweating, repeatedly. As soon as they had climaxed, within five minutes, Celia wanted it again,

"Oh, make love to me, James. Harder."

This went on for about three hours. At five p.m., they collected their possessions and walked out of Room 201. Celia handed Metz some money to pay the hotel bill and a dollar to Guido to give to his friend, a local actor, who played the role of the clergyman. They walked to their car and placed their possessions in the trunk. Metz now walked over to Celia's side to open the door for her. Metz resumed his normal position behind the wheel when Celia leaned over, hugged his arm, and whispered,

"I love you; I love you with all my heart, but you must swear on my life that you will never, ever tell a living soul about what happened today. Do you swear, darling?"

"I swear, my Celia, I swear it."

CHAPTER THIRTY-TWO – ELOCUTION

Chelsea Village, Manhattan

Horace Harmsworth pulsated about his Chelsea Village studio apartment. He dusted and re-arranged the furniture, tucked in the corners of his bed, and cleaned his bathroom. He removed a picture of a couple of Bolshoi male ballet dancers over the toilet. Instead, he substituted a picture of two cowboys lassoing a steer. He threw a red towel over a foot stool to hide its pink color and removed two blue feathers poking out of a mauve vase. He gave a last look at the appearance of the room and breathed a sigh of relief when he heard a knock on the door.

"Metz, James Metz," he intoned, "I'm so glad you could come. Please, come on in and make yourself at home." With one move, Harmsworth swept Metz' jacket off his shoulders and placed it on a hanger. Metz looked around, uncertain of where to go and what to do.

"Would you like me to sit here?" Metz said, and he indicated the kitchen chair.

"Oh no," Harmsworth laughed, "I don't want you to sit just yet. You're not tired, are you? Not too long a walk, yes? Your deportment, first, my dear, before we get around to speech. One must know how to stand before one sits."

"What does 'deportment' mean?"

"Your behavior, your way of acting, your way of conducting yourself, your way of standing, your deportment, voilà, my boy." Harmsworth made a deep reverential bow, as if he were the lead character in a Molière farce. "I'm going to turn your world around, my dear. In just a few easy lessons. You said you're not too tired, yes? So, first lesson. Watch me."

Harmsworth swung away from Metz in the cramped studio. With his left hand on his stomach, Harmsworth pushed it so that it was flat. Then, Harmsworth tilted his chin up with his right index finger so that he looked at the top of the door. Like a bird, he cocked his head from side to side until his brown eyes came to rest on Metz.

"Now, you try, may I call you James?"

"Oh sure."

"You can call me Horace, James. Now, go ahead and walk like I did."

Metz held his head up and walked deliberately around the room. Harmsworth was all over him immediately.

"Very good the way you're holding your head up, but you need to stand straighter, James, pull your shoulders back, imagine your shoulder blades touching, and your chest opening up to the touch." And with that, Harmsworth had his palm on Metz' stomach. "Flatter, James, keep your stomach flat." He kept his hand on Metz' stomach as Metz sucked in his gut and tried to do as his mentor said.

"Like that?" said Metz, and he moved away from Harmsworth.

"Even flatter, James," said Harmsworth. He now had his right hand on Metz' stomach and his left index finger poking between Metz' shoulder blades. "Pull them back, make them touch, James."

"How's that?" said Metz, again moving away from Harmsworth. The acting coach eyed him critically and smiled but said nothing.

"Practice, my boy, practice. Practice makes perfect, that's what they say. Keep going and I'll watch you."

Metz did so, and rapidly improved his 'deportment' as he walked about the room. When Harmsworth was satisfied that his shoulders were back, his stomach was flat and his chin was elevated enough, Harmsworth barked, "James, a big breath in on the count of "one"; now, don't move your shoulders, and a long breath out and make it last to the count of '1-2-3'. Voice, James, put voice in your breath. Go 'ah-h-h-h-h'."

"Ah-h-h-h-h," went Metz, almost with a sigh. "Very good, James, "Say 'ahh' several times." Metz did so. Harmsworth turned into Henry Higgins.

"James, say the vowels A-E-I-O-U."

"O-H, Y-E-H!"

"No, James, not 'Oh Yeah,' A-E-I-O-U." Harmsworth went over to Metz and put his right finger on Metz' lips to stop him from speaking. The teacher then pronounced the diphthong /ey/ or "A" in exaggerated fashion, opening his mouth and closing it during the length of the vowel. "/E-e-y-y-y/. Make it last, James, make your vowels longer, lo-o-n-g-g-er."

"/E-e-y-y-y/" went Metz, and Harmsworth placed his right index finger above Metz' upper lip, and his thumb on Metz' lower lip. "Now do the "E" vowel," and Harmsworth made his vowel very long like he had with "A" and said, "/i-i-j-j-j/."

"/I-i-j-j-j/," imitated Metz, as Harmsworth— clearly enjoying himself—spread and elongated his pupil's lips with his fingers to get the desired effect.

In painstaking fashion, Harmsworth went over all the vowels several times until he was satisfied that Metz could reproduce them properly. The drama teacher often kept his hand on Metz' stomach, then moved his fingers to Metz' lips. "Repeat after me, 'I must articulate.'

"I must ar-tic-u-late," said Metz in exaggerated fashion, "ar-tic-u-late."

After about thirty minutes of this, Metz was exhausted and said, "You got a glass of water, Horace?"

"Better to say, 'Do you have,' or 'May I have' a glass of water, Horace?" said Harmsworth, and he finally let go of Metz stomach and lips. "Please, have a seat. You've played along very well here. What I'm asking is not easy."

Metz sat down while Harmsworth fluttered about. He brought Metz a cushion for his back and one for himself. Then, he brought Metz a large glass of water, and sat down close to him.

"James, what you need now is to create a special character, something that makes you memorable. Something that only you would say, and that people remember. What do you think? Hmmm. I have it! You should call other people, 'Old chum.' Yes, that's it. 'Old chum.'

"Old chum" said Metz deliberately, "Old Chum?"

"Make 'chum' long like 'ch-u-u-mmm'"

"Old Ch-u-u-mmm'" said Metz.

"Very good, Old Chum," said Harmsworth.

JAYNE LOUISE CRAMFORDE AND RICHARD BONTE

CHAPTER THIRTY-THREE – LOVE'S LABOR LOST

Fifth Avenue, Davenport Mansion

James Metz stood at attention as he always had by Mr. Davenport's Rolls Royce on this unusually hot Sunday afternoon. He felt out of sorts for some reason. It had been two days since he'd even seen Celia, ever since their 'wedding' out in New Jersey. It had been a separate and strange 'honeymoon' for both. Her uncle had found an unusual amount of work for him to do on the cars over the past forty-eight hours. He had thoroughly scrubbed his hands, but he could still detect axle grease in the cracks of them. Meanwhile, Celia had remained in her room—as far as Metz could ascertain—for the past two days. At least, he hadn't had to drive her anywhere. He had not been asked to. But just this morning, he had been requested to drive her to lunch at the Oyster Bar in Grand Central Terminal.

What would it be like driving her now? Would it be like before? It was hard for Metz to remember how things had been *before*. 'Before' didn't really mean anything to Metz. There was only the 'now,' the reality of that hotel afternoon by the shore, the lunging, the pounding, the grinding....

And suddenly, there she was. A vision in pink, she wore a large black hat with a long, multi-layered, one-piece dress. It had a wide collar and large pockets. She was all 'cotton marquisette and crepe de Chine,' and she looked stunning. But she said nothing to him, not even 'Hello, Metz.' She just stood on the top porch and looked down on him. *Actually, no.* She looked straight out over him, as if he didn't exist. *What!* She inclined her hat and held her dress with her left hand and majestically walked down the steps. She held her chin up more than usual— was it she who had been taking deportment lessons with Harmsworth? —and nodded coldly to Metz who took her hand and helped her into the back seat of the car. As soon as she sat down, she withdrew her hand quickly and placed it with her other in her lap. He had tried to hold her hand longer than usual to recall their new relationship, but she was having none of it. His eyes smoldered with love as he caught her cold glance, but she cowardly looked away. He stood there stupidly with his hand extended to no one when she cut the silence with,

"Metz. That was not appreciated. Please attend to your business. A driver is hired to drive. Please do so."

Shaking with emotion and rage, Metz resumed his spot behind the wheel when she said,

"The Oyster Bar at Grand Central Station, please, Metz." Her voice was detached and robot-like. Not understanding her new demeanor at all, Metz' forearms shook on the wheel. He pulled out into traffic and headed towards Central Park and over to Grand Central. "Metz, I am sorry, but you must realize what happened the other day is over. One day soon, I will marry for real, and, as you probably understand, it will be to a man of sufficient wealth. And that is all I wish to say on the matter."

Metz' hands tightened on the wheel. His eyes watered with bitterness, but all she could see under her big black hat was waves of heat wafting up from the road.

JAYNE LOUISE CRAMFORDE AND RICHARD BONTE

CHAPTER THIRTY-FOUR – THE OYSTER BAR

Grand Central Terminal

Metz did not bother to leave his seat when he pulled to a stop outside Grand Central Terminal on 42nd Street. Celia hesitated for a moment—she had expected Metz to rush over and open the door for her—but he didn't, so she let herself out and walked over to the Oyster Bar. The New York City landmark restaurant was reputed to have the freshest seafood in Manhattan, even though it was not located on the docks. Established in 1913, it featured a 'Guastavino'-tiled ceiling, with Catalan zigzagging tiles throughout the vaulted ceiling.

Celia saw Don at the other end of the archway in front of the main gold-colored entrance of the Oyster Bar. It was just she and he under the vaulted archway that was known as a "whispering gallery" because its acoustics were so good. Don's back was turned to her, so she decided to test the acoustics and whispered, "Don?"

Don immediately turned around and smiled, "Testing the acoustics, Celia?" he said softly, and moved to rejoin her.

Inside, the tables were decorated in white, with plantation era chairs and ferns, and other green plants. Most of the tables were taken, but the maître d' took the couple to an enclosed alcove on one side that was closed to the public but looked out on the whole floor. It was both private, but not claustrophobic, the perfect table for what Don had in mind. He slipped a five-dollar bill to the maître d' and sat down beside—rather than opposite—Celia, so they could gaze out on the other tables. He wanted them both to feel comfortable in case things did not turn out the way he planned.

The maître d' summoned the various drink and food waiters who then served them a delicious lunch of champagne, lobster and asparagus, seafood salad, and crème brulé. While they sat alone after lunch, sipping cognac and smoking cigarettes, Don turned to face Celia and took her hand in his. She seemed to welcome this, so Don began,

"You know, Celia, I've been thinking about you, about myself, and about us, and we really do get along well, don't we?"

"Yes, we do, Don."

"And we're from the same stock—if you know what I mean—good people who are going somewhere in the world. We could make a great team, you and I, and–"

"Don, are you trying to tell me something?"

"Celia, darling, I am trying to tell you that after these past few weeks, seeing you all the time, that I feel, my life would be, I think that--"

"Oh Don, yes?"

"I just think, that, that the two of us, we have so much going for us, and that, would you marry me, Celia?"

"Oh Don, ohh, oh, I don't know what to say?"

"Say 'yes,' Celia, please."

"Of course, I, don't know what to say, I am so surprised! I'm so young, so innocent, I-"

"Oh, Celia, please, I--"

"We could, you know, Don?"

"Of course, we could, it would be wonderful!"

"I mean, I would have to ask my parents, as well as my aunt and my uncle, but I'm sure, they would be in perfect agreement, they like you so much, can you wait for a moment, for a definitive answer?"

Don had halfway pulled out a diamond ring in a small box from his pocket, but he replaced the box in the bottom of his pocket and said,

"Of course, Celia, this is a big decision for you, a momentous decision. You need to think about it, talk to your aunt and uncle and just have time to get used to this idea, a very good idea in my humble opinion."

Don squeezed her hand and looked lovingly into her eyes. Then, the business finished, he looked up, and waved to the waiter, who came to take his check.

JAYNE LOUISE CRAMFORDE AND RICHARD BONTE

CHAPTER THIRTY-FIVE – BUSTED

Meat Packing District, Lower Manhattan

He liked Charlie, but he didn't trust the other guys in the back seat. They were Goombahs—there was no getting around it—and they might be useful in the short term, if ever he was going to put some money in his pocket. Right now, it was 2 a.m. The Ginzos had their heads down in the back, and any passing cop would think there was just Charlie and he in the front. Metz had shut off the lights in the car when they pulled into Fleischer's Meat Processing Plant. Metz noticed some light at the other end of the street, so he pulled up as far as possible from the light, and as close as possible to the locked door of the entrance. He made sure he would have clear getaway access when it was time.

The three Italians jumped out from the back and attacked the door with a crowbar. They finally snapped the lock. Charlie stayed behind them to supervise. As Metz watched the four criminals penetrate the interior of this processing center, his mind drifted back to when he had first met Charlie, the Italian.

It had been the middle of a hot afternoon. The sun was shining off the Italian's face, turning his yellow eyes into a smoky red color.

"Ninety cents a week."

"What?" said Metz

"You heard me. Ninety cents. Fork it over."

"For what?"

"That's my parking charge for this street," said the Italian. Metz stared at a nineteen-year-old punk, who was looking impudently up at him. Who was this character? There were several kids hanging around the street, but this kid had a lot of nerve. He pointed threateningly at Metz with his left hand, while his right held something in his pants pocket.

"You're speaking to the wrong guy, kid. Why should I pay you ninety cents to park on a public street?" Metz said. He was about to walk away when he saw it come. The right set of a pair of brass knuckles flew towards his face. He ducked and countered with a right hook to the punk's head. The kid dropped to his knees in surprise and saw Metz turn and walk away.

"Hey, Jew boy?" the Italian called out. Metz stopped and turned around.

"I'm no Jew."

*"How come you live in this neighborhood,
then?" Metz saw the kid put the brass knuckles into his
pocket and realized he would no longer be a threat.*

*"If it's any of your business, I live here 'cuz I
want to," said Metz. "And I got a good deal."*

"Hey, listen to me," said the Italian.

"What do you want?" said Metz.

*"I got a deal for you. Join my gang. We call
ourselves 'Five Point.'"*

"Why me?"

*"You're the first guy who did what you did.
You're not afraid of me. I want you on my side. I used to
be a dumb fuck earning seven bucks a week," said the
Italian.*

"That's what I make now," said Metz.

*"That's what I mean. You're gettin' had, pal.
Look at me. I get whatever I want," said the Italian as a
group of five other fourteen-year-olds came up to him,
and, without a word, each gave the Italian a dime. The
Italian nodded to them and then turned back to Metz.
"You see? It's easy. Fifty cents, just like that. I offer
these kids protection against my people and the Irish
gangs. But that's just me and my brass knuckles doin'
the protectin'. I could use a guy like you to help me out.
What do you say?"*

*Metz stared at the kid and realized he could
become an ally or a friend, and not an enemy. He*

extended his hand to the kid, "My name's Jimmy. Jimmy Metz."

"Charlie. Charlie Luciano. Pleased to meet you," said the Italian.

A shot rang out. Metz jumped up from his reverie as three car doors opened and the Goombahs leapt in. Charlie's voice cracked the silence,

"Fuck. He's dead. Get outta here! Quick. NOW."

Metz turned the gas control on the steering wheel on the Model T to 'Full.' Metz floored it as a night watchman ran in front of them with a powerful lantern. Metz just missed the watchman and tore out, but the lantern illuminated Metz' and the watchman's faces. There was no mistaking who it was.

"If we saw him, he probably saw us," said Charlie. Metz sped out of the area. They rode in silence for a few blocks.

"He didn't recognize any of us, did he?" said one of the Italians in the back.

"What do you think, Metz?" said Charlie when Metz stopped to let them out where he had met them. Metz said nothing but stared for a long time into Luciano's face. Then, he drove the Model T back to the 'Polack House' and gathered all his belongings.

CHAPTER THIRTY-SIX – BUYER'S REMORSE

Celia's Bedroom, Davenport Residence

She hadn't bought in yet, but she was about to. Or was she? She had told Don Casterson to give her a week to think about his proposal. She was very young, she told him, and needed time to think about her future. Of course, she loved him, that was not the problem. And she wasn't one to jump into something without reflection. She was a very sensible young woman. She had strong values. She hoped he understood. He had told her no problem, and that he was there for her; he would be there for her, and that he loved her more than ever. And it was that certainty—that Don was a 'bird in hand,' so to speak—that sent Celia to her room for most of the day, because the prospect of a set, never-changing life with anyone, troubled her greatly. Yes, Celia had a decision to make. A very big decision.

Celia had three partners to choose from, and, aside from Metz, they were wonderful marriage partners.

She then remembered Michael Green was supposedly brilliant, but Michael was what he was—there was nothing he could do about it—and that was that. So, there remained Metz and Casterson. Celia fretted that anyone on the outside—like her aunt or uncle—would only see the obvious pick and would understand that Celia had no choice to make. At all.

Besides, she had already 'married' Metz, even though their 'wedding' was ridiculous, and their honeymoon away from each other was fictitious. The point was, Celia had already experienced his love. They had shared the most intimate moments together, so there was nowhere to go but down. Don, on the other hand, was a man on the rise. He had a real promising future, and Celia was dying to experience love with Don as well.

Would it be the same as with Metz? Celia stroked her thighs and abdomen with all the desire of her youth and realized she was a girl on fire. She could no longer think. Her thoughts no longer existed. Rather, they were just flits of fancy under the yoke of blunt lust. Her brain had left her head and was now located 'down there.'

After Celia had satisfied herself, she imagined what life would be with Metz. It would be sexy at first, but at some point, it would turn out awful. Would they live in poverty in a tenement in New Jersey, or would her father give them money to live in luxury? When she put aside her passion, the choice seemed clear.

There was a knock. Celia jumped and opened the door.

"Have you seen Metz this morning, Celia?" said Aunt Betty. "He didn't come in for work. Your uncle needs to go somewhere."

JAYNE LOUISE CRAMFORDE AND RICHARD BONTE

CHAPTER THIRTY-SEVEN – SAFE HOUSE

Chelsea Village, Manhattan, Earlier, at 3 a.m.

"Who's knocking?" said Horace Harmsworth, feeling his way in the dark towards the door.

"It's me, open up," whispered Metz.

Harmsworth looked through the peephole above the door. Metz stood there with two large suitcases. Harmsworth opened the door, and Metz pushed in.

"Close the door, quick," said Metz. "Sorry to wake you."

"What's wrong?" said Harmsworth.

"I have to stay with you. I have nowhere else to go, is that ok?"

"Are you in trouble?"

"Let's just say I had a fight with my landlady."

"We'll talk about it in the morning, shall we, James? Until then, you can sleep in the armchair, or you can stretch out on the bed. You woke me up out of a sound sleep."

"I'm sorry."

"I know you are, James, but I have to go to bed."
Horace stretched out on the bed, and within seconds he
was asleep. James sat down in the armchair and stared
into the darkness.

Lower East Side, Manhattan, 3 a.m.

Two Model T police cars drove up to the "Polack
House." Lefty Goldstein, the night watchman at
Fleischer's, and four policemen jumped out. Drawing
guns, they followed Lefty up the steps; Lefty let himself
in with his key and showed the policemen Metz' room.
The door was wide open, and Metz wasn't there. Three
of the officers raked through everything belonging to
Metz.
"Lefty, what is all this racket?" said Mrs.
Lubelski, shuffling in. She was dressed in white pajamas
and a sleeping hat, and she addressed herself to the
officers. "Careful, you're going to wake up my tenants.
What's going on here? And where is Metz?" she said.
"Mrs. Lubelski," said one of the officers. "Your
tenant's been involved in an armed robbery at Fleischer's
Meat Packing Plant. Unfortunately, one of the security
guards was killed, and Lefty here says Metz was driving
the getaway car."
"Someone was killed? And you think my Jimmy
did it? Go on," said Mrs. Lubelski. She whipped around

to face Lefty. "What are you telling lies for, Lefty? You two never did like each other, did you?"

"Is that true, Mr. Goldstein?" said the cop who had addressed Mrs. Lubelski before. "That you and Mr. Metz are enemies? Are you sure that the man driving was Metz?"

"He almost ran me over in that Model T," said Lefty. "He was as close to me as you are to Mrs. Lubelski here, and I saw him with the light of my lantern."

"Mrs. Lubelski, do you know where Metz is? Why is he not in bed sleeping?"

"All I know, Officers, is that Jimmy Metz always pays his rent on time, and that he is a very nice boy, isn't he, Lefty?" She turned to the officers, "I have no idea where he is, Officers. Can you come back in the morning?"

"I'm sorry, Mrs. Lubelski, we'll have to search the premises. Now."

JAYNE LOUISE CRAMFORDE AND RICHARD BONTE

CHAPTER THIRTY-EIGHT – LOVE'S LABOR WON

Aside from helping Auntie Betty and the cook, Celia had not left her room for three days. And Metz had not been to work in that same time. Where was he? Celia felt his absence had something to do with her. Maybe he had felt embarrassed when he saw her? Maybe he had felt completely emasculated, especially as she had convinced him to tell no one what they had done, and she was of a higher class than he. But why would he have foregone his pay? He was not a rich man. Why would he have just left his job? It had been several days since his 'wedding' to Celia. If he had felt embarrassed, he would have manifested his discomfort immediately, not after a few days.

Whenever she thought of Metz, which was most of the time, she could only think of her carnal needs and the way he made her feel. But there was something else about him that she liked. He was humble, gentle, in a gauche sort of way. Invariably, she would compare him to

179

the two other men she had dated. Aside from money and status, Metz was far superior to both. However, he was *'verboten'* to her because he was poor. Why couldn't she have anybody she wanted, whenever she wanted? She was Celia Dawes, after all. Life wasn't fair.

A lot of things weren't fair. Her uncle had once explained that Life was a pie of dung that one had to swallow slice by slice. The papers had reported that down in Rutgers Square, from Broadway to the Bowery, even to City Hall, poor mothers—many carrying babies—demanded to see the mayor. Their life wasn't fair. All they wanted was food for their children. And all Celia wanted was Metz. She decided she would find him and bring him home.

She went into her closet and pulled out a pair of bloomers. She tried them on in front of the mirror, shook her head, and went back to the closet. She pulled out some olive-drab, knee-buttoned pants, a skirted blouse, a pair of lace-up high boots and a red, plaid tam-o'-shanter. She put these on, ruffled up her clothes, let her hair hang untidily from under her tam, and dirtied her face somewhat with her make-up. Then, she checked her look out in the mirror. She was now perfect to mingle amongst the lower classes.

Celia slipped outside without seeing anyone and took a taxi downtown to the Bowery. The taxi driver had let Celia off two blocks from her destination because the police had cordoned off the area.

"Do you know the Lower East Side? Be careful, Missus," the driver said as Celia paid her fare.

"Ahhh sure wi-ill," said Celia, affecting a slight southern accent.

Celia walked the two blocks to the Bowery with increasing interest and apprehension. She could hear shouting and the neighing of horses. Then she turned the block and heard chanting. A heavyset matron about thirty waved a baton and led a group of other militant women in the chanting.

"Pound of potaters was 2¢. Now, they wants 7¢."

"Pound of cabbage was 2¢. Now, they wants 20¢." Celia tried to speak to one of the marchers. "Do you know Jimmy Metz?" she yelled above the din.

"Is he one of the crooks?" the marcher shouted back. "They're making us starve, you know!"

"No, he's not one of the crooks," Celia answered.

"Well, how do you know, woman?" said the marcher. And with that she picked up a piece of rotten apple and threw it at a police horse. It hit the horse in the cheek whereupon the animal bolted, veered towards them, and knocked Celia unconscious to the ground. The marcher didn't seem to care, and continued to chant, "Pound of potaters was 2¢. Now, they wants 7¢." A passing policeman rushed to Celia's aid. There was blood streaming from the back of her head. He turned her over.

"Do you know who this is?" he said to the marcher.

"Nahh, doesn't look from around here, though. Look at her dainty hands."

The policeman carried Celia to a waiting police ambulance that sped her to the hospital.

CHAPTER THIRTY-NINE – THE CHASE

Chelsea Village, Manhattan

"Would you please pass the salt, James?"

Metz considered his new 'roommate'. Not only was Metz hunted by the New York Police Department, he felt hunted by the overtly homosexual British theater coach across the table. But what could he do to ward him off but give his acting coach compliments?

"The omelet's very good," said Metz as he passed the salt to Harmsworth.

"A little more salt, as well as a bit more pepper and Colman's mustard," said Harmsworth, "will make it very much better. Wouldn't you agree, James? Pass the mustard."

It was Harmsworth's British accent—/betahh, pahhhss/ for 'better' and 'pass'—and his formal ways that Metz had trouble with. It was Harmsworth's studio, not his, but already Metz felt the pressure of Harmsworth's avidity. There was no free lunch, and

Metz wondered what he could do for Harmsworth other than *that,* yes, *that* which could not be named.

"You know, you can stay here as long as you want, James," said Harmsworth flirtatiously. "I mean, you *did* say you were only driving the getaway car, and the others didn't mean to kill him, but that it just happened, isn't that so?"

Metz didn't like this talk, but it was true. Metz felt that the NYPD was seeking the wrong man.

"I mean," said Harmsworth, "I don't consider myself to be harboring a fugitive, but that is sort of what I'm doing, isn't that so?" he said in his professorial, English way.

"I just wanted money, Horace. Not your money, obviously. And I don't want to cost you any money or make any trouble for you. That's why I wanted to know if you could teach me to act like a businessman. I really appreciate you lettin' me stay here for a bit. When I get rich, I'll make it up to you in spades."

Just then there was a thump on the door and Metz jumped. "Oh, don't worry, James," said Harmsworth, "that's just the paper being delivered. He always throws it at the door to wake people up. Anger. Probably figures since he had to wake up, everybody should be awake. I'll get it."

Harmsworth looked through his peephole before opening the door. The delivery boy had left, and so Harmsworth picked up the paper. "Well, look what we have here," said the acting coach. He showed the front page to Metz. "Right under the war news. That's right, right there." He pointed to a small headline at the bottom of the page. "It looks like Davenport's niece — you work for George Davenport, yes? —has been taken to the hospital."

"What?" said Metz, "Celia? Celia Dawes? Is she alright?"

"Seems so," said Harmsworth. "Look, it says right here, 'Celia Dawes, the eighteen-year-old debutante and niece residing with railroad magnate, George Davenport, was knocked down by a horse and taken by ambulance to the Salvation Army Hospital on East 12th street.'"

"But is she alright? That's what I want to know," said Metz, tearing the paper out of Harmsworth's hands.

"It doesn't say," said Harmsworth, taking the paper back and skimming the article again.

"I have to see her. I must find out for myself."

"Oh James, please don't go. The police might notice you. You're so good looking, and now you're wanted for being an accessory to murder," said Harmsworth.

"Horace, you don't understand. I have to go. I'll be careful, I really will."

And with that, James fled the studio and ran out into the street.

Metz kept his head down and walked quickly. He made his way through Chelsea Village over to the Salvation Army Booth Memorial Hospital. From a distance, Metz observed the entrance. He saw a guard there, so he decided to enter the hospital by a rear door that was unmanned. Metz quickly ran up the staircase. Hoping to see where Celia might be, he carefully opened the doors to the wards on each floor.

On the Fourth floor, he chanced upon a nurse who said, "Yes, Miss Dawes is in this ward. But she's had a bad fall and she's sleeping. What's your name?" Metz was unsure of what to do, but as there did not seem to be any risk in telling her his name—and because Celia would not have allowed an unknown person in—there would have been no point in giving a false name.

He ventured, "Metz." A policeman who was standing out of sight, but within earshot, reacted when he heard this. He consulted a notebook with the morning's "wanted briefings." The cop saw the name 'Metz,' which he also remembered from reading the New York Times that morning. He came into view and approached Metz.

"Just a moment, sir," he said. Metz turned and ran as fast as he could down the stairs and out of the building. He ran down the street and was about to stop running in the belief that the cop had not followed when he heard a loud, "That's him."

He heard the shout from behind and wheeled around the corner onto Broadway. Fear cascaded through his body. He did not bother to look around to check who had shouted. He knew the cops were on to him. He accelerated.

"After him," yelled the cop.

Metz noticed a car stopped at an intersection. He pulled the driver out, jumped in behind the wheel, and sped off. Police in a patrol car on the other side of the street made a U-turn to give chase. Metz tried to throw off his pursuers by driving down alleys, but now there were two police cars, and they were gaining on him. He headed for the docks.

At Pier 20 he took a big gamble. He drove straight off the dock into the Hudson River. He figured he would extricate himself and hide behind the floating car before it sank. The cops would think he had died.

The car plunged into the cold murky river and started to fill quickly with water. He had done well to hold on to the steering wheel to not smash against the dashboard during the fall, but now his foot was trapped. It had gotten wedged under the foot pedals. The water had reached his chest and was moving up to his neck.

The two policemen in the patrol car got out, walked over to the edge of the dock, and searched the water for some sign of the driver. All they saw was the car sink into the river. After two minutes they said, "There's nuttin' here, fellas. He's dead."

Meanwhile, two other police squad cars joined the first. The eight cops involved turned briefly away from the scene to decide who would call a tow truck, who would dive into the river, and who would call the ambulance.

CHAPTER FORTY – INDISPOSED

Salvation Army Hospital, Chelsea Village, Manhattan

"Miss Celia? Miss Celia?"

Celia Dawes heard a knocking on the door. She did not feel well. She had been to the toilet twice that morning and felt hot and nauseous. She also had this bad taste in her mouth. Fortunately, she hadn't broken any bones from her fall after the horse ran into her. She had regained consciousness in the ambulance.

The nurse opened the door. "I've come to check your temperature, darling," the nurse said.

"I think I have one," said Celia. The nurse confirmed her fever.

"You're right, Miss Celia. It's 101°. You'll need to stay here at least until tomorrow to see if everything is ok." She was holding the morning's *New York Times*.

"By the way, Miss Celia, I don't want to upset you, but the USA declared war on Germany."

"Pardon?" said Celia.

"The USA declared war on Germany today, April 6th," said the nurse.

"That's terrible," said Celia.

"Yes, I know. Here is some aspirin and a glass of water for your fever. Make sure you drink plenty of fluids and sleep. I'll check in with you later, dear."

The nurse left the newspaper on the bed. In screaming letters, the headline read, 'USA declares war on Germany!' Celia did not read the article, but did register the date of the newspaper, 'April 6, 1917.' She glanced at her diary again as if to note that it was indeed the sixth day of April. *I'm late!*

Belching and feeling her head, Celia flipped the front page of the paper and noticed a small article on page three. It mentioned a police car chase from the Salvation Army Hospital where she was, to Pier 20 on the docks where a wanted man had driven his car into the Hudson River. The name of the driver, 'James Metz', jumped out at her. Celia feverishly finished the article to make sure she hadn't misread. Although they hadn't recovered the body yet, they had pronounced James Metz dead.

CHAPTER FORTY-ONE – THE GOOD SAMARITAN

One Day Earlier

The car was filling with water fast, but Metz's foot was still stuck under the accelerator. Metz told himself to breathe and not panic. He took a deep breath, plunged down and extricated his foot from the pedals. Then, he shot up through the open window of the car that was now completely submerged in the river. Metz swam underwater for as long as possible. When he finally reached the surface, he had traveled twenty yards past the car and the pier. He began swimming to the Jersey side. He could see it from where he was, and he also knew it was a little over half a mile away. He glanced back at the cops who were talking together and no longer looking out over the river.

Hampered by his clothes in the freezing river, he alternated between the breaststroke, freestyle, and swimming on his back. He was happy to still be alive, but the cold water was tough to bear. He hoped he had made the right choice. *Maybe if I start swimming faster, I'll get there faster and I'll keep warmer. But I'll need to conserve energy for the end.*

There was quite a current that was taking him downstream, so he needed to swim at an angle to the current to get to New Jersey as fast as possible. The cold was playing tricks with his mind because he felt the Jersey shore was closer than it was, but then it would recede into the distance again.

***

Geri Southern was happy. She had spent the day as a tourist on ferries to Brooklyn and Staten Island. She had just boarded her final ferry from Union City, New Jersey back to Manhattan. There had been nothing of special interest to see in Jersey. She just enjoyed being on the water.

"Excuse me, young man?"

Geri turned around to see a middle-aged woman pushing a baby carriage and wanting to get past her. Geri smiled and allowed the woman to get by. Geri looked at her own reflection in the window. She was impressed. She was a good-looking young man.

Suddenly there was a yell. "Look, someone's drowning."

Geri ran to the ship's rail and saw a man face down in the water. But when she looked closely, she noticed he was holding onto a log and his face was out of the water. Was he drowning or not? She hoped he was still alive. She looked from side to side in the hope that someone would take action to help this man. However, no one seemed prepared to do anything. Geri dove into the water. She swam to the man, turned his body over to see if he was alive, and towed him to shore.

The man stumbled as he tried to stand. Swaying from side to side, he finally made it to his feet and ran away. He never thanked Geri for saving him.

Geri made her way back to the ferry dock. She felt proud of what she'd done but knew she could never tell anyone about it. The last thing she wanted was publicity as a man.

JAYNE LOUISE CRAMFORDE AND RICHARD BONTE

CHAPTER FORTY-TWO - JERSEY IS BETTER

Hoboken, New Jersey

Metz awoke suddenly. It might have been five thirty or six a.m.; he wasn't sure, but he was shivering outside a hangar in an industrial area. He shook his head and massaged his cold arms and legs. His clothes were still wet, and he was not sure what to do.

In the half light of early morning, he could see some industrial zone workers gathering near the hangar. He made his way round the back before they could see him. He was a fugitive now, a wanted man with wet clothes, and running on an empty stomach.

He walked and walked until the light came up fully. He found himself in central Hoboken in front of a café. He remembered he had fifty cents in his pocket, so he pulled his hat down low and grabbed some breakfast.

Jostling each other and speaking in loud voices, a group of U.S. Army soldiers bustled in. They sat down at a table near his but didn't take any notice of Metz since he looked like a bum. After five minutes, another group of Army personnel joined the first group. One of the soldiers threw a copy of the morning's paper on the table near Metz. He noticed the date of April 7, 1917. The headlines mentioned that President Woodrow Wilson had not only declared war on Germany, but he had also wanted major recruiting to take place immediately. When Metz noticed a third group of Army soldiers come in, he looked outside to see where they were coming from. The U.S. Army draft center was right across the street. He looked at the headlines again, then back at the men, and understood that he was all alone in the world.

***

It was almost his turn at the head of the line. They were a dirty lot, standing single file in front of a long rectangular table where three U.S. Army generals looked them over and signed them up. Shivering with fear and paranoia, Metz kept his head down in case anyone recognized him. He took a deep breath and tried to relax his stooped body.

Then it was his turn, "Step forward, young man," he heard. Metz tried to stand straight, puff out his chest and pull in his stomach. Just as Horace had taught him.

"Name?"

"Metz," he mumbled.

"What? I didn't hear you," the sergeant barked. Metz looked outside and saw a sign across the road. It read, 'Masters Leather.'

"Masters," Metz said.

"First name?"

"J-James, sir."

"Well, Mr. JAMES Masters, what kind of work do you do?"

"I'm a driver, and a car mechanic, sir."

"Wonderful. That's what our modern army needs. Well, Private Masters. Welcome to the United States Army. You're lucky. You'll soon be taking in the delights of Paris, France."

JAYNE LOUISE CRAMFORDE AND RICHARD BONTE

EPILOGUE

Maui, Hawaii, Eight Months Later

A couple of ceiling fans blew hot air over the receptionist, a nurse, and Celia herself, who was clad only in a long, simple, white cotton dress and a wide-brimmed black hat. In some cultures, white was the color of death, but in the west, black represented that color. And that's how Celia felt today, in both black and white, as she observed the 'little something' mewling in the nurse's arms opposite her. It was perfectly shaped, very handsome, and what was more important was that the child was hers.

"Don't worry, Mrs. Metz, your son will be well-looked after until he is adopted by one of our wonderful families." Mrs. Metz began to cry. "Please, I know it is always so difficult when a natural mother cannot afford to raise her child."

With her grave demeanor and lips drawn tight around her lying mouth, Celia told another series of fibs

199

as she signed the final adoption papers. Then, she arose and kissed her baby one last time.

"Good-bye, my love, James Metz, Jr." And to herself she whispered, *"Maybe God is on their side."*

Celia burst into tears and ran from the room.

THE END

ALSO, BY RICHARD BONTE:
Novels by Richard Bonte & James Crew Allen
Grand Cayman, Exposed

The Wuhan Tentacles

The Baja Redemption

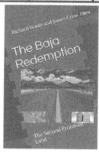

Novellas by
Richard Bonte & James Crew Allen
The Moses Story, or
(The Second Promised Land, Book Two)

A Pact with the Devil

Novella by Richard Bonte
Skeletons in the Closet

Novella by Richard Bonte and David G. Lee
I will "Prey" for You, My Love

Novels by Richard Bonte & Hamilton Harcourt Fleming III

Black on White: The Roaring Twenties

All Black: 1930's Hollywood Secret Lives

The Three Cousins

Novels by Richard Bonte & Jayne Louise Cramforde
The Sisters

The Sisters by Bonte&Cramforde, ███

The Sisters by Bonte&Cramforde, ███

Sisters

Sisters by Bonte&Cramforde, PRINT&E-BOOK

Novels by Richard Bonte

Curmudgeonly Yours

Terry's Upside

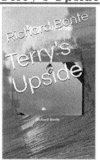

Against Nature: Waste

The Tennis Bubble

Short Stories by Richard Bonte

Curmudgeon in McDonald's

From Muslimia to Tattooland

The Tattooed Server

The Choice

Short Plays by Richard Bonte

The Empire One-Act

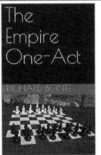

Smarter Than You: Trump Derangement Syndrome Run Amok

Made in the USA
Middletown, DE
07 July 2022

68673681R00119